The
Out Crowd

By Michael A. Kirby

The Out Crowd

Michael Kirby

ISBN (Print Edition): 978-1-09830-229-0

ISBN (eBook Edition): 978-1-09830-230-6

"*In the land of bleating sheep and braying jackasses, one brave and honest man is bound to create a scandal.*"

-Edward Abbey

5

TABLE OF CONTENTS

Chapter 1: Break-Up

At Gates High School, everybody was split cleanly down the middle into two groups: the In Crowd (population sixty-nine) and the Out Crowd (population one thousand and twenty-four).

It was a cloudy August afternoon near in tail end of a hot summer, on the last weekend before school started. Isaiah, a senior Out Crowder, rushed to school as fast as he could. When he arrived, he rushed down to the football field and rushed up the bleachers to get a good view of the field. Isaiah was often forgetful, but today he had set a personal record. He had forgotten today was the final scrimmage before Homecoming. He had forgotten today was not a good day to oversleep. He had forgotten what the best time to set his alarm was to avoid oversleeping. He had forgotten he needed to get his ticket to the Homecoming Game. He had forgotten he also still needed to get his ticket for the Homecoming Dance.

"Over here," Everett called out to him. "Did you oversleep again?" Everett was a skinny senior with a beaver-brown crew cut. He had been one of Isaiah's best friends since the fifth grade.

"I guess so," said Isaiah.

Craig butted in. "You guess so?" Craig was another senior boy with sunflower-blond hair and an arm tattoo of a tree with an infinity sign crafted at the center of the branches. He was Isaiah's other best friend. "You're such a clown sometimes. Did you at least remember to book your Homecoming tickets?"

"Yes," Isaiah said, nodding awkwardly. "Well, I remembered that I still need to book them," he clarified. "I haven't actually booked my game ticket or my dance ticket yet, but that doesn't matter. I'm going to get both now while we watch the scrimmage." Isaiah reached into his pocket, but his insides froze. He had left his phone at home. "Umm…any chance I could borrow one of your cells?"

"Not mine," said Everett. "I'm using it at the moment to download the *Gates Times* app."

"Our school newspaper has an app?" said Isaiah, surprised.

"Of course," said Everett. "It's the current year. Everything has an app now. I thought I would write for the *Times* again this year, to spruce up my college applications. Are you still trying for that scholarship?"

"Yes," said Isaiah. He had a phone interview scheduled with the Jefferson Lee Scholarship Fund at four o'clock sharp tomorrow afternoon. That was one thing Isaiah could count on remembering. He had been studying their requirements since the beginning of August, but he couldn't think about that now. His tickets were his immediate concern. "Craig, can I borrow your phone?"

"Won't do you any good," said Craig. "It's out of battery."

Now he needed to find someone else's phone to use. It was too late to go back home and find his. Isaiah scanned the crowd and his eyes settled on Karen. "Great." Karen was Isaiah's ex-girlfriend. "I'll be right back."

"Is he going to talk to Karen?" said Everett.

"This ought to be good," Craig said, smirking.

Coach Ericks took a deep breath and blew his whistle to signal that the scrimmage was about to begin. "Come on, boys," he yelled. "Hustle, hustle, hustle." He watched carefully as all the teenage boys at varying stages of growth and puberty marched past him. "Joel," he said, taking his senior captain aside when he strode by with the others. "As usual, we've got a lot of freshmen new recruits this year. Make sure you set them straight."

Joel Boudin nodded curtly. "Understood, Coach."

Senior cheerleading captain Hallie Flynn also positioned herself accordingly. There was not traditionally much to be done in the way of cheerleading during a scrimmage, it was true, but Hallie truly believed practice made perfect. This wasn't really just any scrimmage, either. Next weekend was Gates' Homecoming Game against Byzantine High School, and this was their last practice beforehand.

Hallie approached her position as a cheerleader with as much dedication as Joel Boudin. Hallie Flynn always set the mood of the cheerleading squad from the top down.

This pivotal scrimmage attracted a fair bit of an audience. Members of the Out Crowd took their seats in the bleachers: upperclassmen, underclassmen, nerds, wannabes, drifters, emos, those who traveled in packs and even those who considered themselves full-blown outcasts stopped by.

"How stupid of me," Isaiah whispered to himself. Registration had been open all summer, but he hadn't even downloaded the app. "Hey Karen," he said when he was standing right in front of her.

Karen turned to see who interrupted her conversation with the other senior girls she was with. "Hey Isaiah," she reciprocated.

"I wanted to ask you about Homecoming."

"Isaiah, we broke up in April," said Karen. "Don't you remember?"

"No, it's not that," Isaiah said quickly. "I need to book my tickets, but I left my phone at home."

"Oh Isaiah, you haven't changed."

"So I was wondering if I could borrow your phone for a second," Isaiah requested, "to book my Homecoming tickets." Truthfully it would take longer than a second to get done.

"Well," said Karen. She sighed deeply. "Alright."

Isaiah was relieved. "Thank you Karen. I really appreciate it."

"Whatever. Just hurry up."

Isaiah scrolled from screen to screen and back again. "I can't find the app."

"My school app crashed the other day," Karen told him. "You probably need to re-download it."

"Ugh, fine." He clicked the download button. "It says it'll take a few minutes."

"A few minutes?" Karen took her phone back and looked at the screen. "It must be the reception. Here, I'm gonna check my messages. Go back and sit with Craig and Everett. I'll come by when it's done."

Isaiah had no choice but to do as she said, but he couldn't stop himself from getting anxious. This was taking way too much time. Then again he was partly to blame.

Summer weather was still in the air, and t-shirts and shorts were the norm amongst returning students. Isaiah,

Craig and Everett were not the only ones in hot anticipation of Homecoming. How the team performed after a summer of training was usually a good indicator of how hopeful their classmates and fans could be in the upcoming season.

"Can you believe this is our senior year already?" said Craig. "It seems only yesterday that we were all sitting here as freshmen."

"I know," said Isaiah. "I think the three of us have seen every game together."

"Not the one before the PSAT last year," Everett pointed out. "We all had to study, remember?"

"And I missed a game sophomore year," said Craig. "The one where I had mono."

"Fine," said Isaiah. "Every game but two. Do you think Gates will reach the Western County finals again this season?"

"I don't know," said Everett. "Brett Webster already graduated, so we need fresh talent to stay competitive."

Craig stroked his chin. "Brett was the best star quarterback Gates ever had. Now that he's at Big City University the county playoffs will be tough."

"We're playing Byzantine High in Homecoming next week," said Isaiah. "We'll see what happens then."

"Evan Terrence is Byzantine's captain now," said Everett. "He'll give us a run for our money."

"He's not unbeatable," said Craig. "Don't forget we still have Joel and the rest of the seniors. All of them have an extra year of experience now."

"Meh," said Everett.

"I just wish that I could get a better look at the field," said Isaiah. "Hallie's on top of her pyramid so I can't see the kickoff."

"Surprised she's even practicing that of all things now," remarked Craig. "The ground's muddy so it's easier for those holding her up to slip."

"Well, that's part of what they have to do," replied Everett. "Some game days are muddy or rainy, and they don't have a choice then. So why should they stop practicing on a scrimmage day?"

"True," Craig conceded.

Karen swung by and interrupted their conversation. "Here Isaiah." She handed her phone back to him.

"Awesome," said Isaiah. "Now I just need to register myself and send the ticket to my email. First I need to make an account. Let's see. Pick a password. Then click next. Oh, it's asking me to enter the password again."

"Hit the back button," said Karen. "And pick something you'll remember long enough to enter it a second time."

"I wasn't expecting to have to enter it again," said Isaiah, irritated.

"What about when you need to sign into your student account for other stuff?" said Karen. "Did you think of that?"

Isaiah ignored her question. "I don't know what's going on. For some reason I can't send the tickets to my email address."

Karen snatched her phone back. "Let me see. The reception must be having trouble. I'll see what I can do. Oh drat!"

"What?" asked Isaiah.

"I clicked the wrong button," explained Karen. "Now your ticket's file is saved to my account and I can't scroll back."

"Oh," said Isaiah. "I guess I'll have to come to the Homecoming Dance at the same time as you, since both our tickets are on your phone."

Karen rolled her eyes. "Fantastic."

"It won't be like we're going to the dance together," Isaiah said, "because we're not. We can just arrive together, show both our tickets on your phone and then go our separate ways."

"I know Isaiah," said Karen. She seemed to regret agreeing to help him earlier.

"Thanks, Karen." Isaiah felt awkward about it as well.

Karen waved to Craig and Everett. "Hey guys."

"Hey Karen," said Everett.

"How was your summer?" she asked.

"Pretty good, Karen," said Craig. "Yours?"

"Mine was fine," said Karen. "My mom dragged the family on vacation and there were millions of bugs where we went. I got bit way too many times, but I survived," she explained, with a slight laugh in hindsight. Karen perched herself into a seat between Craig and Everett. "So, did you guys hear about Hallie and Brett breaking up over the summer?"

Craig widened his eyes in astonishment. "No," he said.

"You've got to be kidding me," said Isaiah. "I thought they'd both be at the dance next weekend."

"I actually did hear they broke up," said Everett, lacking his friends' surprise. "Didn't they break up right before Brett left for BCU?"

"Yep," Karen confirmed. "That's not all, either."

"It kinda makes sense," said Isaiah. "Brett's off to college and Hallie's still in high school."

"Actually that really wasn't it," Karen corrected him. " I'm sure Brett would've come back for Homecoming, but summer was pretty rough for them. He wrote a long, angry break-up letter to Hallie which later got posted in a blog."

"Wow," Everett said with a hint of a laugh. "I definitely didn't hear about that part. What was in the break-up blog?"

"Too many things to keep track of," said Karen. "Apparently Brett felt used in the relationship, said she cheated on him a couple times, ranted about her supposed conflicts of interest with the school…"

"What do you mean conflicts of interest?" asked Isaiah. That sounded sketchy, whatever it referred do.

Karen shrugged. "That's what it says in the blog."

"What were the conflicts of interest though?" said Isaiah.

"I don't know," Karen admitted. "That's just the phrase Brett used in his post. It doesn't say what they are." She typed on her phone. "I'll send you guys the link."

Hallie stumbled and shook on top of the pyramid. The girls beneath her shifted in an attempt to keep her feet balanced, but their struggle was futile. Hallie wobbled back and forth and finally, she fell from the top of the pyramid and landed face-first in the mud. Joel called a time-out and rushed over to help her to her feet. Hallie stood up slowly, her uniform drenched and her hair and face soggy. She could have sworn she heard a few laughs in the distance, but she could not tell whom they belonged to. Undoubtedly, they had to be from somebody in the Out Crowd.

Chapter 2: Homecoming

That evening the In Crowd gathered at the Asteroid Pizza, a local hot spot. Joel ordered a dozen large pizzas for the gang and the owner offered them a substantial discount. The owner had done a lot of business with Flynn Telecommunications and Hallie's father owned Flynn Telecommunications.

"That was a good scrimmage," Joel said, half to himself, half to Hallie and the rest of the senior first string. "I think that we're going to beat Byzantine easily."

"That's awesome, Joel," said Hallie. "Don't get too cocky, though. Their new quarterback this year is someone to watch out for."

"Relax Hallie," said Joel. "Did you see how many fans came to see us today? We're gonna kill it, and everyone knows it. You should try not to be so nervous, or you may fall again." Joel noticed her glaring at him. "I mean, never mind. It could happen to anybody." He averted his gaze. "None of my business."

Hallie took a deep breath. "I was distracted."

"What were you distracted by?" asked Joel.

"I don't know," Hallie said, trailing off. Then she decided to get out what was really on her mind. "I think some people were talking about…the note."

"Ah," said Joel. Hallie had tried to get whoever posted a blog with Brett's break-up note to delete it, but even if they had it wouldn't have mattered. The entire school probably knew by now, and the damage had been done. "You know how kids are," he said to Hallie, choosing his words carefully. "They talk about one thing one day, and then they talk about something else the next. It'll die down soon."

"I don't know about that," said Hallie. One gossip cycle always flowed into another gossip cycle. "They've been talking about it for quite a while." The break-up blog had been posted well over a month ago. Brett had accused her of cheating on him with two other guys, having said guys promote her election for cheerleading captain and participating in numerous "conflicts of interest" during her time at Gates High.

"I didn't hear anyone mention it recently," said Joel. "Maybe it's people just getting back from summer break being brought up to date by their buddies."

Just then, the pizzas arrived and Joel took some time to sort them out between dozens of cheerleaders and football players. This caused a long interruption his conversation with Hallie.

With a little more time to think it over, Hallie let out a deep sigh. "Yeah, I suppose you're right, Joel," she said. "Even if this gossip is targeting me, I can't let myself be distracted by it any longer. Maybe none of this would have happened if I hadn't been so open with my ex-boyfriend, or if I'd acted differently on our final date."

"There you go, Hallie." Joel smirked as he took the biggest piece of pizza with the most toppings for himself, then sat back and let his fellow seniors divide the rest amongst them.

For a moment that seemed to settle the matter, but just then one of the other football players decided to speak up. "No Hallie," said Jarvis Edwards. "You're wrong."

"Excuse me?" said Hallie, raising an eyebrow. She hadn't interacted as much with Jarvis as with other members of the In Crowd. Jarvis had only just joined the team last season, and many suspected he had earned his spot in the second string by offering to get the team's average GPA a boost.

"This isn't your fault," said Jarvis. That got Hallie's attention in a good way. "I know what I'm talking about, Hallie, and you can't give in and blame yourself for this. The real problem is the toxic environment at Gates High. That's what allows rumors like that to form in the first place."

"What?" asked Joel, trying to follow what Jarvis was saying.

"A toxic environment?" Hallie repeated. "What do you mean?"

"The break-up blog, whoever posted it, the kids who talked about it, the kids who laughed and distracted you today, it's all part of the same thing," said Jarvis. "It's a toxic environment and that's what's throwing you off. You need to stay strong and not allow yourself to fall prey to the toxicity."

"What are you rambling about, Jarvis?" Joel asked through a full mouth of pizza. "Is this something you heard in one of those courses you took over the summer?"

"Yes," nodded Jarvis. "I did take some college-level classes, so like I said I know what I'm talking about. Hallie, it's not a matter of having a bad day or being distracted. This is all part of a toxic environment, and it's trying to keep you down. You need to rise up against it!"

"Huh," said Hallie, considering the idea. "You know what Jarvis? I think you're right. This can't be my fault – what happened over the summer or what happened at practice today. It's this toxic stuff, yeah. And if it's not my fault than it must be somebody else's!" She slammed her clenched fist down so hard her soda nearly fell off the table.

"You are so totally right, Hallie," said one of the younger cheerleaders. She smiled and nodded in agreement, along with the other two sophomore girls next to her. Granted, none of them had actually listened long enough to know what they were agreeing with, but they had all noticed the upperclassmen's conversation had just grown louder and more important-sounding than their own.

"Hmmm?" said Joel, tuning back in after tuning out.

Hallie turned back to him, now much more engaged. "Jarvis was just telling me the real problem that happened today. It's not that I was distracted. The reason that I fell was because of the toxic environment at school."

"If you say so, I guess," said Joel. "How do you mean?"

"Toxicity can do that," said Hallie. "I want to know who was causing this to be toxic so that I can make them pay!"

"Whoa, slow down," said Joel. "You just fell when you got distracted. It's not like I've never been too distracted before. Is that toxic, too?"

"I don't know," said Hallie. "Maybe."

"Look, let's all just try to stay focused for Homecoming," said Joel. "We'll make sure that you and everyone else here is on top of their game. Let's just turn the negative into a positive."

"Well…" said Hallie, trailing off. In truth, she was no expert on toxic environments the way that Jarvis was, so she was a little uncertain how they worked in her limited personal experience. "I suppose that you're right about that, Joel. Even so, I do wish that I knew who these toxic people were. I'll show them for laughing at me behind my back."

* * *

Gates High School had seven wings - six for each major subject plus a visitor center - and a swimming pool. The two-story brick building was just spread out enough to box in its eleven hundred students. The football field was adjacent to the building with the swimming pool.

On the Saturday of the Homecoming game, the In Crowd all took Joel's advice. This included both the football players and the cheerleaders. Hallie Flynn found her spirits lifted a little when she saw how the stands filled up. She beamed, but one of the junior girls had the nerve to remind her that it would not be like that all season long. Anyone who was anyone at the school attended Homecoming Games, but during the regular season people were less interested. Unless the team made the Western County finals, of course, but even then there would only be a crowd from their side if it were a home game.

"I'm doing what Joel said," Hallie told her. "I'm turning a negative into a positive."

"Whatever," the junior cheerleader rolled her eyes. "Why don't you just move on from what went wrong at the scrimmage?"

"Nothing went wrong at the scrimmage."

"You fell."

As she shooed the girl away, Hallie did not hesitate to say she would not allow her to do the new move they had planned along with everyone else. "Serves you right." The junior girl snickered, but Hallie ignored her.

Joel Boudin joined the referee and Evan Terrence from Byzantine High School. The Gates High School logo was neatly painted in the middle of the field where they gathered. Stands lined the sidelines, with the Gates spectators in front of the locker room and the visitor stands at the opposite end, beside the woods.

Byzantine High School won the coin toss, so Gates kicked off to them and Joel managed to tackle their wide receiver and pin him just before the 40-yard line. On the whole, the first half was a really slow game, with neither team scoring any touchdowns. Hallie took it upon herself to maintain the audiences attention.

As usual, she climbed to the top of the pyramid and smirked when she reached the top. Then, on purpose, she hopped down and plunged face-first onto the ground, her head landing right on target in the nearby mud-puddle. As soon as she was out of the way, the two girls who had been holding her up hopped down themselves and landed in the exact same puddle of mud. Finally, the girls who had been at the bottom holding them up followed suit. This new cheerleading "move" the girls had invented was apparently called "the Splat."

The Out Crowders were unsure of how they were supposed to react. Hallie frowned when her performance drew silence and confusion rather than applause. At least her fellow cheerleaders were supportive, yelling in unison for Hallie to perform an encore, all of their own noses still browned by the mud.

Their fearless leader followed suit and Hallie dunked her face into the muddy ground once more, so it was even more covered when she brought it back up again, with only the spaces around her mouth and both her eyes showing.

The Homecoming Game picked up in the second half. Joel scored the first touchdown of the game midway through the third quarter. Joel Boudin was not timid in his touchdown dance. He shook his hips, drum-rolled his arms and even did a couple of cartwheels to top it off. After almost a minute, he finally returned to the huddle. The referee waited a moment to make sure he was done before blowing his whistle. Coach Ericks shot Joel a disapproving look, but then congratulated his star player on Gates' first touchdown of the season.

The dance earned a few laughs from the audience, though it was understandable why Joel would be so elated. It was the first touchdown of the season, after all. Later on Joel tackled Evan Terrence, Byzantine's captain, just as he was about to intercept the ball. Joel did a shorter version of his dance then.

Gates High School had a seven to zero lead, but the rest of the game was much more competitive. Both coaches yelled at the referee at least five times apiece. At the close of the fourth, Gates edged out Byzantine by a simple field goal, winning the game seventeen to fourteen. Byzantine's captain was very bitter on the outcome. Since they had both had winning seasons for the last five years, there was a good chance that Gates might face Byzantine in the county finals in November.

Joel Boudin even considered that a certainty. "We'll be seeing them again," he told the rest of the team as Evan Terrence and the others boarded their bus.

* * *

The Homecoming Dance was held in the Gates High gymnasium and the decorations had been put up by the underclassmen that afternoon. To nobody's surprise, Hallie was chosen for Homecoming Queen and Joel received the title of Homecoming King. Many had expected Brett Webster to reappear from Big City University as Hallie's date, but since they had broken up over the summer this did not happen. Hallie had gone stag to the dance.

Joel came with his girlfriend, the freshman Veronica Morgan, but they arrived several minutes late, just in time for Joel to be crowned along with Hallie. Promptly, Joel rushed over, leaving Veronica behind, as he took to the floor with Hallie in the first dance of the evening, all eyes on them. They had the opening song to themselves. Hallie's shining peach-colored Homecoming dress complemented her long blonde hair perfectly. As soon as the first song finished, others started dancing as well.

The music grew louder and the true fun of the night began. Most of the Out Crowd onlookers finally got over their disappointment of not seeing Brett Webster again, even the most diehard of football fans.

"Are you going to ask Karen to dance?" Everett asked Isaiah.

Isaiah looked over at Karen. She had a nice dress on. "No, I think that'd be too awkward for both of us."

"Suit yourself," said Everett.

"You should dance with someone else," Craig suggested to Isaiah. "It's Homecoming. Have some fun."

"I suppose you're right," said Isaiah. "But who?"

"Well I guess you can ask my cousin Claire," said Craig.

"I didn't know you had a cousin here," said Isaiah. "She doesn't live in town, does she?"

"No," said Craig. "She goes to Byzantine High, but she got asked here by one of our second string football players. He's currently puking in the bathroom. Too much pre-gaming."

"Wow," said Isaiah. "And the dance just started, too."

"Yep," said Craig. "Now my cousin's all alone. And so are you."

"Go for it," Everett agreed. "It's perfect timing. Just don't talk to her about our football teams' rivalry."

"Well...okay," said Isaiah.

Craig introduced Isaiah to Claire and he danced a couple songs with her. Everett went ahead and danced with Karen himself.

Once this initial round was finished and everyone around them started dancing as well, Hallie insisted that Joel dance with her a little longer. Joel consented to this.

Meanwhile, Joel's date Veronica hung out near the back of the dance hall with the other ninth grade girls. Some of them had come with dates and some on their own. They asked Veronica who she had came with, and she told them Joel Boudin was her date, but the other freshmen girls didn't believe her. They had just seen Hallie and Joel dance together in the opening. The other girls proceeded to laugh at Veronica.

It was near the end of the evening when Hallie finally released Joel. He immediately rushed back to his actual date, but Veronica no longer felt like dancing.

Chapter 3: Cafeteria Exchange

The events of the weekend were still being universally talked about the following Monday. As usual, Hallie Flynn and Joel Boudin were the centers of attention. Now, though, the teenagers were not speaking of the break-up blog post at all. They still talked about Hallie falling on her face, but it was on her own terms this time. Additionally, the Homecoming dance, as well as Joel's dancing antics on the football field made it a very memorable opening to the school year.

After Hallie's demonstration of her new move on Saturday, a handful of underclassmen cheerleaders decorated their noses with dirt before coming to school, to mimic how Hallie looked after performing the Splat. No one else picked up on it, so they failed to start a lasting fashion trend.

"Well," Craig said through a bite of his tuna sandwich. "This is an interesting start to the semester."

"Certainly a game we won't forget anytime soon," said Isaiah. "I would've enjoyed it more if Joel stayed more focused on playing and less on his touchdown dance."

Everett rolled his eyes. "There's sometimes no pleasing you Isaiah. Say, what did you think of the Splat, Isaiah?"

"Honestly," said Isaiah. "I think that it's the stupidest thing I've ever seen."

"What?" Confused, Everett scratched his short brown hair. "Why are you giving Hallie such a hard time? Is it because she's so pretty, and popular?"

"Do you really need me to explain why I don't like the Splat? Use your common sense."

"I just hope that this craze dies down soon," said Craig.

There was a clear divide in how students reacted to the events of the weekend. A majority of the kids at Gates High School didn't spare a second thought on the Splat once the game was over. The second-largest group thought it was stupid and were laughing at Hallie and the cheerleaders when they were not around. Then there was the smallest group of kids, who openly took her side at all times. Hallie decided this group had to be emboldened.

Joel's advice had not helped. People were being more toxic than before, and that made Hallie annoyed at him. She would do things her way from now on.

Greg Goldstein had arrived early to homeroom that day. Only he and a few other kids were present. "Say, did you guys hear why Hallie covered her face in mud?" Greg asked the others in a hush.

"I dunno," said Roy Wilson. "Why?"

"To cover up all of her zits," said Greg. Everyone was still laughing when the rest of the homeroom poured into the classroom.

"What's so funny?" asked Phoebe, a cheerleader. She was busy munching down a muffin she had just grabbed from the breakfast line in the cafeteria.

"Hallie did the Splat to cover up her acne," Marcus, her boyfriend, informed her. He eyed the rest of the newcomers, but none of them laughed the way everyone had before.

Greg leaned toward him and whispered in his ear. "It's all in the delivery man."

Phoebe smiled politely as she took the seat next to Marcus. "It was a good joke Marcus," she assured her boyfriend.

"Just not good enough to laugh at," Isaiah muttered to himself. Unlike the rest of his homeroom, Isaiah remained at his desk, reading up on the requirements for his scholarship program.

"I'm a little worried about Hallie," Phoebe confessed to Marcus. "A lot of people are going to be talking about her again today. She sounded really upset over the weekend."

"Whatever," said Marcus. He noticed Phoebe's scowl. "That comes with being the center of attention. She'll get over it."

"I guess so," said Phoebe. But she sounded uneasy.

Sally Smith was a plump and pimply junior. She ate lunch with two other girls in her year, but Friday was the only day of the week they all ate lunch together. They had separate lab lunch days for chemistry class. One of them had lab lunch on Monday and Wednesday, the other had lab lunch on Monday and Thursday and Sally herself had it on Tuesday and Wednesday. Today was Monday, so Sally expected to eat lunch by herself.

Out of the corner of her ear, Sally heard Roy Wilson and some other kids in her grade making fun of Hallie's Splat move. Like a funny cat video, the novelty wore off faster for some people than for others. "You guys are such jerks!" she shouted. "Knock it off."

By sheer coincidence, at that moment, the In Crowd was just leaving the lunch line and about to take their seats. Hallie heard Sally and approached her. "Hey, it's Sarah, isn't it?"

Sally gulped. "It's Sally, actually," she corrected her, though she was nodding quickly as she said it.

"Sally, alright," Hallie acknowledged, her lip curling. "Thanks for telling those guys off."

"It's nothing," said Sally. "They were ridiculing your performance at the last game."

Hallie smiled. "Why don't you sit with us today?"

Sally Smith's eyes widened. "What? Are you serious?"

Joel turned to Hallie. "Yeah, wait, what? Are you serious, Hallie?" He turned to Sally and saw he had not lowered his voice enough for her not to hear "I mean, yeah, sure. That sounds awesome."

The cafeteria at Gates High was an enormous diamond with the lunch line on one end and the vending machines at the opposite corner. Isaiah, Craig and Everett had sat at the table closest to the vending machine since their freshman year. Meanwhile, the In Crowd clustered around the tables at the center of the room. Hallie Flynn and Joel Boudin always sat at the very center of the center. Anytime Hallie and Joel were absent, the senior cheerleaders and backup linemen relished the spotlight for themselves.

After accepting the invitation, Sally took her seat at the long table, surrounded by football players and cheerleaders. "This is so cool," she whispered under her breath. Everyone around her had still not gotten over the surprise themselves, so they quietly played along, waiting for Hallie or Joel to clarify what was going on. Of course, Joel himself was also waiting on Hallie for that.

The mass of school colors clustered about the central tables now had a blank spot. Sally Smith sat there in normal clothes - neither a cheerleader's outfit nor a football uniform. "That was a great move that you did at the game on Saturday," said Sally, smiling broadly, as she addressed Hallie.

"Thank you," said Hallie, not bothering to look up from her tray.

"And good job on getting those touchdowns, Joel," said Sally.

"Thanks," said Joel, not making eye contact.

"Same goes for the dance you did after you got the touch-down," she added. "The Splat was awesome, too. It makes me want to be a cheerleader myself some day."

Hallie smiled. "That's nice. I don't think you have the body for it, my dear."

Sally asked questions, the boys gave short, direct responses, and the girls ignored her as much as possible, except for Hallie herself. For the most part, the table was quiet, and everyone seemed uneasy, with the exceptions of Sally and Hallie.

After half an hour of awkward lines, the lunch bell rang and the time came to disperse. "So, that was fun," said Sally, though it seemed like she was the only one who had fun. "I've got lab lunch tomorrow and Wednesday. Can I sit with you guys again on Thursday?"

Not only Sally's, but also every pair of eyes on the table fell on Hallie now, waiting for an answer. She was the one who ini-tiated this, so she was the only one in the know. "Perhaps," said Hallie, almost bored, examining her painted nails. "But you'll have to do us another favor before then."

* * *

That was how it all began. From Sally's case, word spread fast and many members of the Out Crowd from all parts of the school started doing favors for the In Crowd. The In Crowd's favorite favor was simply saying good things about them. Shouting someone down who was saying bad things about the In Crowd was also appreciated. Either one of these was a guaranteed ticket into the new "sit with the In Crowd for a day" program. Sitting at their tables also came with the added benefit of being *seen* sitting there.

It expanded pretty quickly. Before too long, every day at lunch the In Crowd's tables had several "guest faces" sitting amongst them. They typically had to bring some extra chairs over from other tables in order to accommodate. Visiting members of the Out Crowd had the opportunity to feel like they truly were somebody important, even if it only lasted for half an hour at lunch. People would compete for seats next to Joel and Hallie, or sometimes go for a corner seat, so that the people they normally hung out with would be able to see them. Or so their enemies could see them and they could brag to them later.

Some boys and girls of the Out Crowd decided that they couldn't get enough of it after sitting with the In Crowd one day, so they rushed to do another favor for them as soon as possible. The In Crowd always asked for a little extra on the second time around. If saying one nice thing about Hallie in homeroom was enough to get lunch with them the first day, the second time Hallie might expect them to start a rumor about someone that the In Crowd hated. Gossip cycles were going by fast, so hardly anyone could keep track of all the rumors spreading around school.

One junior boy, Jimmy Hugo, was with them every single day, though he only took his seat with them halfway through lunch. For fifteen minutes he would stop by every other table in the lunch hall one at a time, smile, wave and do an extended bowing motion. Sometimes he would quote lines from one of his shows. Jimmy was in Gates' theater program, and he played the lead in the school play Hamlet. As the most popular kid in school who was not a part of the In Crowd proper, he found ways to constantly stay on their good side.

During the showings of the school production of Hamlet, Jimmy would ad lib lines to fit with Hallie's narrative of the school. "To be or not to be, that is the question, but there's no question about the toxic environment here at school. Toxicity sucks!"

Another recent line of his was "There more things in Heaven and Earth, and the toxic environment here in school, than are dreamt of in your philosophy."

Of course, Mr. Wheeler and the other instructors who ran the Gates High School theater program were angry whenever Jimmy did this. They would say things like "you should be more professional," "not the time or place, Jimmy" or simply "don't say lines that aren't in the script." But Jimmy was a personable, well-liked guy and he always managed to talk his way out of it, even while being scolded after every performance.

"Besides," he reminded them. "You shouldn't talk like that. People may think that you're helping those who are toxic, too." They did not understand how this was the case, but they dropped the subject.

Chapter 4: The Gates Times

Further into September, Hallie approached Shelly Boudin, Joel's twin sister who was Editor-in-Chief of the *Gates Times*. Shelly arranged for a meeting after school between herself, Hallie and Mrs. Friedman, the *Gates Times* faculty advisor. Mrs. Friedman was a veteran teacher with short hair and glasses, who had taught at Gates High School since long before any of the students or even some of the other teachers were born.

Mrs. Friedman always took a picture with herself and the student newspaper staff at the end of every year. The wall of her office was lined with dozens and dozens of such photographs going back to the late sixties. Now, the wall of her office was lined with dozens and dozens of such photographs. Mrs. Friedman looked pretty much the same in every photo, as though she were timeless herself. No one knew Mrs. Friedman's exact age since she never told anyone. Rumor had it she even sealed any school record that mentioned her birth year. She had to be much older than fifty-five now, so one could say Mrs. Friedman looked very good for her age. Then again, everyone must have said the exact opposite about her when she was a young woman.

"Good afternoon," Mrs. Friedman greeted as she sat down behind her desk and gestured to a pair of chairs in front of her for Hallie and Shelly to sit in.

"Thank you again for meeting us, Mrs. Friedman," said Shelly. "I know your schedule's a busy one.

"Not a problem," said Mrs. Friedman. "What can I do for you, girls?"

"It's Hallie's new idea I mentioned the other day. We wanted to discuss it more."

"Right," said Mrs. Friedman, nodding. "Well Hallie, I'd like to thank you for taking an interest in us. From what Shelly tells me your idea would be...well, quite a change."

"Change that needs to be made," replied Hallie. "The football fans gave me the idea for it."

"I think she has a point Mrs. Friedman," said Shelly. "This is for the best, given how toxic the climate at school has become."

Mrs. Friedman clicked her tongue with unease. "Generally only those who have contributed to the *Gates Times* for a while make drastic changes to how we do things," she told them. "If you want to contribute, Hallie, that's great. We have a lot of writers already and our newspaper fills up fast with every issue, but I'm sure we can find some place for you. Before you start your own regular article series, though, it's customary to write a few assignments to become a regular writer first. For your first assignment, why don't you interview one of the newly hired teachers about-"

"Oh no," Hallie cut her off. "I'm sorry, but I'm afraid I'm far too busy with my cheerleading to write for the *Gates Times* myself. It was an idea I had that I'd like someone else to write. I was talking about it over dinner the other night and my dad thinks it's a good idea, too."

Mrs. Friedman raised an eyebrow. "Do you have anyone else in mind?"

"She doesn't yet," Shelly answered for her. "But that's no problem at all. I can find someone to write Hallie's idea for an article no problem."

Mrs. Friedman took a few seconds to ponder this. "I still have my reservations."

Shelly swallowed hard before responding. "As I said before, Mrs. Friedman, I can find the writers to contribute to Hallie's new idea. We have plenty of stellar newspaper staff. That will not be a problem."

"I know all that, Shelly," said Mrs. Friedman. "It's the idea itself that's giving me reservations. The topics you want to cover don't fit our standards for articles. Furthermore, these subjects can't be verified as factually correct."

"I know it's mostly speculation," Hallie admitted. "That's why we're calling it a gossip column."

"It's not news," Mrs. Friedman said flatly.

"Sure it is. It's just a different kind of news," replied Shelly. "You can't pretend it's not part of student life. Kids spread rumors all the time."

"Yes," Mrs. Friedman conceded. "I know that kids gossip all the time, but it's not something that we typically want to promote as a school. I'm sure that Guidance Counselor Bethany would agree with me. There's been quite an epidemic of rumors lately. Principal Terrence is actually considering hiring a second guidance counselor for the school. Rumors can cause a lot of damage, and that's a danger we need to take seriously."

"I know, Mrs. Friedman," Hallie interjected. "Trust me, I've been the subject of rumors myself, so I know not just how damaging, but how toxic it can be. Knowing people are out there making fun of me is devastating."

"Right," said Mrs. Friedman. "So why do you want to add in a 'gossip column' now? That will spread rumors about other kids."

"Because I've realized that's the only way to really make the problem better," answered Hallie. "Kids spread rumors all the time behind each other's back and it gets out of hand pretty fast, but with a gossip column in the *Gates Times*, the school paper could lead the student body to a better way of doing things. Everything would all be out in the open, centralized and nice and neatly organized for everyone to follow."

Mrs. Friedman's eyes lit up. "Wow, Hallie, you know I've never thought of it that way, but that sounds really bold and forward-thinking of you. I promise I'll give this some serious consideration and get back to you sometime next week."

"Next week?" Shelly repeated. "But Mrs. Friedman, the next issue comes out tomorrow. Can't you let us give it a go sooner?"

"Will you even be able to add a gossip column in soon enough?" asked Mrs. Friedman. "That seems like quite a time crunch."

"I can do it," said Shelly, brushing her hair back behind her head. "I've dealt with deadlines before."

"Besides," said Hallie. "A couple of girls already gave drafts of their first pieces when they overheard me and Shelly talking about it."

Mrs. Friedman let out a deep sigh. "Very well. Give your new idea a test run, but be sure you aren't late with the new issue, Shelly."

"Relax Mrs. Friedman," said Shelly, smiling in triumph. "You can count on me."

Following the meeting, Shelly rushed straight to the *Gates Times* office. She and Deputy Editor Zach O'Phant spent the remainder of the afternoon rearranging the issue. She had a few gossip columns drafts, which she needed to find a place for before the presses ran, but it turned out that the issue was already full. Shelly needed to economize.

Finally, she came across four items to clear out. An article about English teacher Ms. Eden setting up a local charity to fight childhood leukemia was replaced with "Roy Wilson Has A Unique Fart Sound, So You Can Always Tell When It's Him." A guide on preparing to take the SAT was replaced by "Cindy and Simon Break Up for the Fourth Time." Shelly also took out an article written by Yazidi, the new girl, about the War in Yemen. Three articles, along with the funnies section were scrapped and tossed so that Shelly could make room for the debut of the *Gates Times* gossip column.

Art Teacher in a Coma?

Summer fever is now over and the school year is underway, but Ms. Monet-Marbleton, the art teacher, has been absent so far. It is not confirmed yet whether Ms. Monet-Marbleton will be returning at some point or if Gates High School will have substitutes teaching art class indefinitely. Whatever the reason, her continued absence is impossible to ignore. Since she obviously cannot be reached for comment, this has become a topic of much speculation.

Prevailing gossip claims that she succumbed to a coma before school started.

If this is true, we cannot expect to see Ms. Monet-Marbleton for some time. The question also remains how she came to be in a coma in the first place. Rumor has it that she was in a traffic accident. Additionally, some students were present when it happened. More recently these teens were laughing at one of Roy Wilson's joke about Hallie Flynn.

Imagine for a moment that Ms. Monet-Marbleton had her accident because she could not shake her frustration at the toxic behavior of Gates High Schoolers nowadays. Yes, she has been missing since before that happened, but perhaps there was some prophetic wisdom in the timing of her accident. It would explain a lot.

"Wow," Everett said as he read the article aloud. "I never saw it that way. Isn't that thought provoking?"

Isaiah stared at him. "No, no it isn't."

Everett didn't back down. "What are you talking about Isaiah? Were you listening? The article is right. Ms. Monet-Marbleton has been absent and this would explain a lot."

"Her absence has nothing to do with Roy," Isaiah replied, shaking his head.

"You don't know why she's absent!"

"Whatever the reason, I'm sure 'toxic' people bothering Hallie Flynn have nothing to do with it," said Isaiah. "That's connecting imaginary dots with an imaginary line."

Many students had thought the new issue was a joke at first. They weren't used to reading about how some underclassman boy never wore boxers (Howie Goes Commando Every Day), the valedictorian from last year cheating on every test (How She Really Did It) or an urban legend of someone installing cameras in the school bathroom.

Some of the students only ever looked at the funnies section, so they were most disappointed when their only purpose for reading the school newspaper was taken out, and they quickly lost interest. Others were in sheer disbelief that blatant gossip was allowed in the school newspaper. The kids actually in the gossip columns were in a precarious position. Everyone could read whatever it was that was said about him or her, student and faculty alike. It was only a matter of time before their parents and families knew what was being said about them, whether it was true or not.

Ordinarily when someone was targeted so maliciously, they would go to the principal, but unlike the blog of the leaked break-up later, this gossip was fully backed and endorsed by the school newspaper and by extension the school itself. Most of those who were mentioned pretended to ignore it. Some went to Guidance Counselor Bethany or the new hire, Guidance Counselor Griffin.

"I understand that some might find it distressing to have all these new rumors," Hallie conceded. "It's just the price we pay for a less toxic place to go to school." She had made the front page herself, under the headline "Splat, the Best Cheerleading Move of All Time."

The biggest gossip at Gates High a week before was Brett Webster's break-up blog post, but that wasn't covered in the

Gates Times gossip columns at all. One article, however, covered similar incidents.

> Breaking Gossip: Anita Patel, freshman, found an online post from her former boyfriend detailing his woes in their relationship. The post appeared only thirty minutes after they had broken up via text message. Naturally, Anita was shocked at the detail he went into.
>
> "He said he was dumping me for the fourth time," said Anita. "But we've only broken up and got back together twice." Apparently blogs like this are not to be trusted.
>
> Anita's not the only one, either. Tammy White, senior, confirmed with the *Gates Times* that her boyfriend did the same thing following their break-up.
>
> "I didn't realize Tammy White had broken up with her boyfriend," said Anna Mason, sophomore.
>
> "I didn't even know she had a boyfriend," said Gary Jackson, sophomore.
>
> Is this a new epidemic? No one knows yet. A handful of similar incidents have been reported in our gossip cycle. Most were unable to be reached for comment, but all have occurred within the past twenty-four hours. Tammy White's was the most recent to come to our attention. Despite some unsavory gossip to the contrary, no other senior

cheerleaders are confirmed to have such blogs posted about them.

In the front section (not the school activity section) Shelly Boudin herself published a glowing review of the school production of Hamlet.

Go See Jimmy Hugo in Hamlet

When I went to see Gates High School's production of Hamlet, I was treated to a spirited performance of my peers. From start to finish, it was a gentle progression which must have taken a lot of effort, but seemed to be effortless. Jimmy Hugo takes a bold approach to this Shakespearian tragedy. The audience can tell his purpose is not merely to perform a play but share his viewpoint. He does not shy away from doing this whenever an opportunity arises. Overall, Gates High's production of Hamlet this year brings a moving message clothed in a masterful performance. With Gates High star Jimmy Hugo eloquently adding his modern contributions to an old story and a stunning cast in general working together, this is a school play that no student at Gates High ought to miss.

Jimmy of course boasted about the review in every conversation he had, whether it was with In Crowd, Out Crowd, or teachers. "If the play was so great, why was the auditorium only half full?" people would sometimes ask him. Jimmy Hugo would always just ignore it.

"Keep calm and brag on," was Jimmy's new motto. He boasted about Shelly's flattering review even in completely unrelated circumstances.

"Who can tell me what year the Declaration of Independence was signed?" Mrs. Friedman asked in history class. "Jimmy."

"1776 was the year it was signed. And today was the day the *Gates Times* reviewed my play. Shelly Boudin said it was awesome."

"Good for you, Jimmy," said Mrs. Friedman. "Karen, will you put your phone away please?"

Karen looked up. "Hmm?" She had been glued to her cell phone when Mrs. Friedman asked the question.

"Put it away before I confiscate it," said Mrs. Friedman, now annoyed with two of her students. "Now, moving on-"

"The next showing is this Thursday evening," Jimmy announced, interrupting his teacher again. "Tickets are on sale now and can also be bought online at GHS dot Western County dot E-D-U." Even with Jimmy's constant self-promotion the current showing of Hamlet still had some of the worst attendance of any play in Gates High School production history.

Jimmy had other problems on his hands as well. After the last showing, Mr. Wheeler was at the end of his fuse.

"Stick. To. The. Script," Mr. Wheeler spat at his lead actor. "Seriously Jimmy, how hard is that for you to do? I have had enough of your defiling a work of Shakespeare with your petty school gossip."

"Sorry Mr. Wheeler," said Jimmy, not sounding sorry at all. "I just can't help myself."

"Listen, you've been a great asset to the program during your time here at Gates, but these irrelevant anachronistic ad libs of yours are just intolerable. Your understudy is a hard-working sophomore who knows all the lines by heart. I'm starting to think it might be time to give him a fair shot."

"But Mr. Wheeler, think of Hallie Flynn."

"This has absolutely nothing to do with Hallie Flynn. This has to do with the integrity of the performance and turning around our declining attendance."

"The same people bothering Hallie are responsible for the declining attendance."

"What people?"

"The toxic people. Remember the rumors that started over the summer, and all the toxic kids around who said terrible things about her Splat move? Hasn't Hallie suffered enough? I'm trying to be supportive of my fellow students during a time of crisis."

"During a play is neither the time or place for such things." Mr. Wheeler was running out of what little patience he had left. "The theater is a time for us to come together, perform a play and invite everyone to watch, regardless of who they are what our differences with one another are outside in the real world."

Jimmy shook his head. "We cannot let the toxic people win."

"Face it, Jimmy," Mr. Wheeler said, getting right up in the junior's face. "Your added lines of dialogue are what's causing our current nosedive in ticket sales." The theater program, which had never been low on funding, was going to have to make cutbacks soon. "Not some invisible toxic people."

"Please, you mustn't say such things," said Jimmy. "That's what the toxic people want you to think."

"No, it's the obvious truth."

"Mr. Wheeler," Jimmy said, raising his voice. "You're not toxic yourself, are you?" That finally shut Mr. Wheeler up. No one at Gates High School, not even faculty, wanted to be thought of as toxic.

Meanwhile, Jimmy continued to sit with the In Crowd kids day after day. As much as he outwardly ignored it, Jimmy was fully aware of the declining attendance and wanted to turn it around. He tried to persuade Hallie at lunch to come to the play herself next time and bring some friends, reminding her of all the support he had given her thus far. Hallie politely told Jimmy that she would think about it, but never followed up.

Joel Boudin simply grunted when Jimmy asked him the same thing. Then he ignored it anytime Jimmy brought it up again.

The In Crowd tables had more and more seats around them with each passing day. As Hamlet's attendance fell, the In Crowd's favors only escalated. Dan, the Treasurer of the Dungeons and Dragons Club, went to a party at the Flynn residence over the weekend.

"Wait a second," one of Dan's friends said as soon as he told them. "You actually got to hang out with them outside of school. What did you have to do?"

"Well, some kids were spray-painting a message saying 'Hallie belongs in the mud' on one of the bulletin boards, so I told the principal," said Dan from Dungeons and Dragons Club. "It was something none of the In Crowd kids could have done themselves, because that would be snitching, but since I'm from the farthest corners of the Out Crowd, I had no problem doing it. The kids all got detention with Mr. Zee the next day and Hallie Flynn gave me credit."

"Wow. That's amazing."

"I know," said Dan, excited. "They let me stay for five entire songs and have one drink there before they made me leave. It was…truly amazing."

Craig chuckled during lunch when he glanced Jimmy Hugo making one of his obsequious monologues to Hallie Flynn. "Wow, this whole 'sit with the In Crowd for a day' craze is becoming quite funny."

"I don't know how funny I would call it," said Isaiah.

"What's with you?" Everett asked him. "You sound troubled, Isaiah."

"The In Crowd's gone to great lengths to get the gossip going their way. The gossip columns are just a small new subsection of the *Gates Times* and the favors for sitting with them for a day are stupidly harmless, but I'm starting to wonder if that's not the end of it. What else will they do?"

Everett scoffed. "Just shut up and eat your lunch, Isaiah. You're paranoid."

Chapter 5: Class Clown

Days passed, and business as usual mixed in with all the new antics going on at Gates High School.

The Gates Times; Volume 69, Issue 5

From the Editor: Changes to the School Newspaper

Many of you have noticed our recent change in tune. I understand that the gossip column section is something most of us are not used to reading. It was not something I envisioned myself not too long ago, but it is called for by the times. When toxic football fans bullied Hallie and made fun of her Splat, I knew something was off and the *Gates Times* had to take on a role of setting the record straight as well as monitoring gossip conversations.

As of today, no one can point out exactly who all these toxic gossipers are but in time we expect to get to the bottom of it. In the meantime, our school journalists have some promising leads. No names will be mentioned yet, but a certain...farter...

comes to mind. More on that another issue. For now, I'd just like to assure the Gates student body that you can count on us to provide good, reliable high school gossip.

Hallie Flynn adores means no harm to anyone. She wouldn't hurt a fly. Truly, she adores all her fans, both In Crowd and Out Crowd alike. But Hallie has been through enough and she needs to set the record straight. Here at the *Gates Times* we likewise care about our school community and want to ensure that the only people who fear the toxic are toxic people themselves.

Let's have a fantastic year everybody!

Shelly Boudin, Editor-in-Chief

It would soon be time to pick the superlatives for the seniors. Elections would be held the coming week in homeroom. Everett, Craig and Isaiah all joked about which one of them would be given Most Likely to Cut Class and Still Get an A, Cutest Couple, Most Opinionated or Most Unforgettable, which were fun topics of conversation, even if they weren't realistic. None of the three of them stood out nearly enough among the senior class to get voted in for one of the superlatives.

Depending on the superlative, it would be won presumably by a member of the In Crowd or the Out Crowd. Jerry, the Captain of the Math Team and Hilda, the President of the Engineering Club were widely expected to win Most Likely to Succeed. One of the writers for the *Gates Times* published an op-ed advocating for Shelly Boudin to be Most Likely to Succeed, but it wasn't taken seriously by anyone, even Shelly herself.

Cutest Couple would go to Bob and Celeste. Most of the time people found them really annoying, but choosing superlatives was a time to give credit where it was due.

Joel Boudin and Hallie Flynn would win Most Popular. No one brought up anyone else as a potential contender for either the boys or the girls, even as a joke.

Then there was Class Clown. Among over a dozen superlatives at Gates, Class Clown soon became the one, which everyone was talking about. The reason was because it was a close contest, at least for whoever the boy would be. Marcus O'Reilly was the In Crowd's favorite. He was a third string football player who was much more well known for telling jokes than he was for his mediocre athletic ability. All of his friends laughed at his jokes and said he would be perfect for class clown, but those who didn't know him were all unable to get his jokes most of the time. Polite smiles were the best that he got from most of the Out Crowd.

And then there was Greg Goldstein. He sat in the back row of class, making witty remarks and vulgar jokes, especially when there was a substitute teacher. Greg was an Out Crowder, and although some of his friends were bullies, he never bullied anyone himself. He was relatable to everyone, and that gave Greg his own unique brand of popularity, which was untouchable, even to the In Crowd.

During the few days before the votes were cast on school superlatives, Hallie would tell everyone at her table how funny she found Marcus O'Reilly's humor, especially the visiting Out Crowders. The day before the vote, Shelly published a new issue of the *Gates Times*, with an endorsement of Marcus O'Reilly prominently displayed on the front page. This was unprecedented. The

Gates Times had never officially endorsed anyone for a superlative in all its decades-long history. Class Clown was getting the most attention and coverage in no small part because it had become regarded as a "swing superlative". Soon, everyone from one end of the school to the other was talking about it.

"So much dramatic tension!" exclaimed Jimmy Hugo. "I wonder what will happen."

"Who cares?" said pimply Sally Smith, annoyed. "It's just one stupid photo in the yearbook. Geez, people make way too big a deal about these things."

"I've thought about it for a while," said senior Karen. "Now I think I've finally made up my mind. What's that?" She was in the middle of writing a text message. "Who am I voting for? That's none of your business."

"This is no contest at all," said Isaiah. "Greg is the blatantly obvious choice for Class Clown. This entire 'swing narrative' is crap."

"I agree with you on this, Isaiah," Craig said to his friend at lunch the day before the vote. "I was thinking about it earlier, but then I realized, there's not much to think about."

Everett bit his lip. "Guys, I don't know about that. The *Gates Times* wrote an interesting piece making the case for Marcus, so maybe we should give him a fair chance."

"Listen Everett," said Craig. "I like Marcus. He's a nice guy and all, but Class Clown is about who makes people laugh more, and that's definitely Greg. Case closed."

Everett grunted. "I guess you're right…" He sounded a little uneasy nonetheless.

The following morning, every student at Gates was given a ballot in homeroom listing all the superlatives in alphabetical order. All of the options were write-in, so technically any senior was eligible for every superlative, though no senior could be nominated for more than one. The In Crowd and Out Crowd alike cast their secret ballots, and waited in anticipation for the announcement of the results that afternoon. It took all day, well into the afternoon for the votes to be counted. Even with the yearbook staff helping on their free time and the principal's secretaries overseeing the bulk of the process, it still meant the results would only be revealed the following day in homeroom.

Despite all the hype around Class Clown being a 'swing superlative', the vote wasn't even close. Greg defeated Marcus by a wide margin. As much as the In Crowd pushed for Marcus, for the majority of the Out Crowd it had never really been a contest at all. Marcus withdrew himself into an unusual state of silence for the rest of that afternoon, while Greg humbly thanked his supporters right before he joined the rest of the winners to take yearbook pictures.

Every picture was a reflection of what the corresponding superlative stood for. Hallie had spent two hours doing her hair that morning for her Most Popular picture with Joel Boudin. For once, she seemed to have forgotten completely about any rumors that concerned her. Joel and Hallie wore a football uniform and a cheerleading uniform, respectively. They stood in front of the bus entrance to the school parking lot. Jerry and Hilda, chosen for Most Likely to Succeed, were garbed formally in a suit and pantsuit respectively, and the two students picked for Most Likely to Cut Class and Still Get an A had their photo taken inside one of the hallways, tiptoeing next to a door as they smiled for the camera. Bob and Celeste sat at a miniature table, with an out-of-season Valentine's Day decoration placed between them.

The photo for Class Clown was taken outside the school. Phoebe, the girl who was elected as Class Clown, joined Greg. Phoebe was Marcus O'Reilly's girlfriend, and she flashed a wide smile that showed all her teeth but did not quite meet her eyes. Greg, meanwhile, smirked and winked at the camera. Then, just before the photo was taken he took a half-step back and held two fingers above her head. The Out Crowd laughed heartily at the bunny-eared photo. Those who did so at the In Crowd table were told to leave.

Chapter 6: Damage Control

The Smoker's Corner was a small area behind the school next to the large dumpster near the soccer field. It was a special place all the kids knew about while none of the faculty did. Students would regularly come outside between classes to smoke and exchange the juiciest of underground gossip.

"Sup fellas," said Angie, a sophomore member of the Outdoors Club. She turned to Brad, one of the other regulars who frequently patronized the establishment. "Can I bum a cig?"

"You always bum," said Brad. He reached into his pack and handed one of his cigarettes to Angie nonetheless. "I think you owe me at least a few packs from last year. Why don't you bring your own?"

"Maybe next time," said Angie. "Can my friend bum one, too? I haven't seen her for a while." Becky and Angie had been best friends throughout all elementary and middle school. When they got to high school, their interests had diverged, but they remained acquaintances on good terms.

"Sure, why the hell not," Brad said sarcastically. He pulled out two more cigs – one for Becky and one for himself, then held up his lighter and lit all three. The Smoker's Corner was about much more than just smoking, of course. The familiar smell of decomposing trash mixed in fittingly with the rabble of trashy gossip. "I heard Marcus is still salty about losing out on Class Clown."

"Yep," Angie concurred, inhaling from her cig. "Not as salty as Hallie, though."

"Hallie is such a bitch," said Brad. "I guess she finally found something she couldn't get with favors."

"To be honest, I'm pretty sure kids are getting sick of those favors," said Angie. "Sure, the whole sitting-with-the-In-Crowd-for-a-day fad lasted for a while, but I think people have gotten sick of it now that the initial excitement over it has died down. Even Hallie must realize that."

"Hah," said Brad. "That's got to be a rude wake-up call for her, then. As far as she knows, everything that doesn't go her way is 'toxic.'"

"Yes, toxic," said Angie. "Toxic, toxic, toxic. I am so sick of that word."

"It's becoming ridiculous," said Brad. "What do you think, Becky?"

Angie's friend simply shrugged and took a long drag from her cigarette.

"She's a quiet one," Brad remarked. "Anyway, Angie, I totally agree. I think just about everyone is starting to see right through Hallie."

"Not just Hallie," said Angie. "There's also the rest of the In Crowd who goes along with it all."

"True," Brad concurred. "Hallie is the one who's addicted to being the center of attention, though. Ever since that blog post, it's all been downhill."

"What blog post?" said Angie.

"Ummm…the blog post where Brett Webster dumped Hallie and started rumors about her. Didn't you see that?"

"Oh yeah," said Angie. "Yes, of course I saw that. Hallie had some 'conflict of interest' or whatever and she cheated on Brett Webster with three or four other guys."

"I think it was something like that," said Brad. "But honestly, I had forgotten all about the blog with everything else going on."

"Rumors come and go," said Brad. "Somehow, Hallie always seems to be at the center of it all. You know, if she had just moved on from that blog post and let it die down on its own, nobody would be trash-talking her now."

"That Splat move of hers didn't help," said Angie.

"Point is, all of the gossip about Hallie now is self-inflicted."

Angie giggled. She had almost finished with her cigarette. "Careful, Brad," she said. "People might start calling you toxic," she joked.

While Angie and Brad had been exchanging gossip with one another, Becky had stood silently the entire time. She contributed nothing to the conversation, but listened closely, taking in every single word and committing it to memory.

Becky was a cheerleader.

Two days later, a new surveillance camera was installed just above the dumpster, and Principal Terrence announced that from now on one of the school security guards would patrol that area a few times a day. The Smoker's Corner was no more.

Smokers across Gates High School groaned at this news, but this reaction paled in comparison when it was revealed who had informed the administration of what went on out there: none other than Hallie Flynn herself. The straightedge kids always steered clear of the Smoker's Corner, but at least they would never tell any of the teachers or staff about it. It was unheard of for anyone to do something so uncool, let alone the queen of the school.

* * *

The lights of the GHS locker room were dim. Principal Terrence had neglected their maintenance the past couple months. Hallie and Joel had to deal with this as they both held meetings there after school. The cheerleaders were in a state, and Captain Hallie had her work cut out for her calming them down.

"I understand what you're thinking," she said, choosing her words carefully. "I've never wanted to stop anyone from going out and enjoying a smoke, but trust me. This had to be done."

"Why?" asked one of her fellow cheerleaders.

"Yeah," said another, even more hostile sounding than the first. "Why?"

"The Smoker's Corner was a very toxic place," Hallie explained. "Perhaps it wasn't always that way, but this year with this disturbing toxic trend taking hold of the school, the Smoker's Corner was becoming easily one of the most toxic places in the school. Toxicity must be met with resilience at all costs and at every opportunity. Becky did the right thing by coming to me the other day."

Becky slumped her shoulders when she was named. She looked as though she regretted speaking up.

Fortunately for Becky, all the other cheerleaders kept their focus on Hallie. "I still don't see what was more toxic about the Smoker's Corner compared to the rest of the school," said one of the new freshman cheerleaders.

"The Smoker's Corner was toxic because of its trashiness," Hallie answered, "and I'm not talking about what's in the dumpster. People spread terrible, cruel rumors there, and they were rumors beyond our reach. I know what people have been saying, but this is not all about me. The hurtful toxicity preys upon us all. I'm not talking about the kind of gossip you'll find in Shelly's gossip columns for the *Gates Times*. These smokers could be saying anything, about any of us, and we wouldn't know about it."

The locker room fell silent as Hallie finished. Finally, everyone agreed that she had done the right thing, and no more was said on the subject.

An hour later, Joel Boudin held a similar locker room conference. If anything, the football players were even more infuriated than the cheerleaders had been. Many of them were smokers themselves. Even when they were in an uproar, all of them looked up to Joel as a leader and an example. Once it became clear that Hallie was insisting the matter be dropped, and several of their girlfriends were following suit, the Gates High School football team realized that they had no option but to drop it.

Until recently the Smoker's Corner had been one of the biggest bridges connecting the two crowds. Now, most of the Out Crowd would not interact with anyone in the In Crowd unless they performed an act of kowtowing to them and got invited to eat lunch with them for a day.

* * *

Besides the Smoker's Corner, one of the largest peripheral hubs of gossip at Gates High School was the cafeteria in the early morning. Every school day breakfast was served starting half an hour before homeroom. The vast majority of students never came to get breakfast at school and the ones that did were of a much different breed than the smokers. There was almost no overlap between the two groups, but regardless of that, there were also some wild gossipy stories that had their origins there.

When the breakfast line opened, the three kids at the front were seniors almost never seen this early: Joel Boudin, Hallie Flynn and Shelly Boudin.

"One bowl of cereal and one small latte," said the lady behind the lunch register. "That will be one and a half lunch tickets." She looked down a second time. "Aren't you going to get some milk for your cereal?"

"Milk?" said Hallie. "Absolutely not. Milk is toxic."

The lady raised an eyebrow. "Excuse me?"

"Ugh, don't you read the *Gates Times*?" said Hallie, condescendingly. "Milk is known to be toxic and having milk can make you toxic."

"Whatever," said the lady. "Can you just pay up and go take a seat somewhere? There's a long line of kids waiting to get their breakfast."

Hallie ignored her. "Any decent person needs to reject toxicity completely. Silencing me on this is an act of violence."

Shelly butted in and held up a copy of the latest *Gates Times* issue, which featured an article on the toxicity of milk. "It is rumored that milk has highly toxic properties," Shelly began reading quotes from the critique. "During our current Age of Toxicity, milk is quickly becoming the symbol of toxic people, a rallying cry for the friends of our toxic environment against the humanity of anti-toxic individuals."

"Shut up," said a junior boy at the back of the line. "Nobody cares. Just get your breakfast and go."

Shelly persisted. "To preserve our character, we must all stand in constant rejection of all toxic people and toxic elements. Toxic people and the symbols they covet stand against all of us and against the interests of our people. It is time for everyone to just say no to toxicity."

Her twin brother Joel spoke up next. "You know, I've been drinking milk my whole life and never thought it was a big deal. Heck, I actually thought it was good for you for a while." Joel spoke loudly so not just the people near him but everyone in the cafeteria could hear. "But let me tell you something, being toxic isn't cool. I will never consume milk again."

Joel and Shelly each got a can of orange juice to pour into their cereal. They seemed to know in advance it would taste weird, but at least they knew they would be safe from any toxins in the milk. One of the gossip columnists for the *Gates Times* had started a rumor in his latest article that milk was toxic and one must avoid it to remain untoxic. Since she ordinarily never came to the school breakfast, Hallie was unsure of how many calories were in the juice, so she simply got a bottled water to pour into her cereal. School breakfast was unfamiliar territory for her, but she was satisfied with her decision to come on just this one occasion. It was an opportunity for her to lead by example, with both of the Boudins there to back her up.

Everyone behind them in line ordered milk for their cereal.

* * *

During that breakfast, some of the students turned on the televisions mounted to the walls in the corners of the cafeteria. It turned out there were professional and college football games on, which attracted great interest.

It was the same at lunch as well.

"Check it out," Craig pointed out to Everett and Isaiah. "Looks like Big City University is about to play one of the state schools."

"Cool," said Isaiah. "We'll get to see Brett play again. It'll be just like the old days." A good old-fashioned football game, pure and simple. No Hallie or Joel showing off. Just a real game played by real people and watched and enjoyed by real people.

"I don't think we'll get to see much of the BCU game," Everett chimed in. "Lunch is almost over. We'll barely have enough time to watch the kickoff."

Meanwhile, the gossip cycles continued. Some kids were on drugs, some were related to famous people, some were dating, some were breaking up and some kids were doing way too many things to fit in one article. A growing trend in the *Gates Times* was for gossip columns to cover collusion with opposing football teams.

The Gates Times; Volume 69, Issue 10

Byzantine High Infiltrates Gates

For most of the past decade, Gates High's primary rival in the Western County football championships has been Byzantine High School. This rivalry has become quite heated at times. Gates High and Byzantine High used to kidnap each other's mascots the night before a game. Five years ago this ill-advised tradition came to an end, when both school principals mutually agreed to crack down on the practice. When the current seniors were freshmen, Byzantine High started a rumor that Gates' quarterback was on steroids, which led to an investigation. Naturally, the claim was unfounded, but it still damaged that quarterback's college prospects. Present-day captain Joel Boudin remembers this well, being a rookie at the time.

Even today, Byzantine High Schoolers are up to their old tricks. They have planted spies among our own students. We cannot confirm how many because most of them have succeeded in keeping their activities secret, but not all of them. Roy Wilson, junior, allegedly met with Evan Terrence, the current star player of the Byzantine High team, and colluded on rigging the next game against Gates in favor of Byzantine. This meeting may very well have taken place last year on Black Friday, at the Western County Mall.

"Did you hear that guys?" Everett asked his two best friends. He had been reading the article aloud during lunch. "It sounds like Roy is a spy for Byzantine High School."

"No he isn't," said Isaiah. "That's ridiculous."

"But he was at the Western County Mall last Black Friday," Everett pointed out. "Several witnesses remember seeing Roy that day. A dozen other witnesses saw Evan Terrence."

"Okay," said Isaiah. "Did any of them see Evan and Roy together?"

"Well…no," Everett admitted. "But why do you keep making excuses for them Isaiah? This is a pretty illuminating coincidence."

"No it isn't," said Isaiah, exasperated. He stopped eating. "Everett, it was Black Friday. Most of the teens in Western County go to the Western County Mall on Black Friday. It's when the best holiday shopping deals are, and the teenagers who aren't shopping get cheap ice cream at the food court. All of these witnesses in the article were also at the mall at the same time as Evan Terrence was. Are they Byzantine spies too?"

"Wow," said Everett. "That's a good point Isaiah. I didn't think of that. Maybe these Byzantine spies are more common than we expected.

Isaiah smacked his forehead. "That is not the point. Everett, me, you and Craig were at the Western County Mall last Black Friday also," Isaiah went on. "Karen was with us, too," he added. Isaiah had bought her a snow cone to redeem himself after forgetting her birthday. "Are you a Byzantine spy Everett? Am I? Are all of us?"

Craig, who had been silently munching his sandwich this whole time, finally decided he had had enough. "Guys let's talk about something else."

"There ought to be a rule against fraternizing with Byzantine High Schoolers," Shelly Boudin asserted in one of her own articles.

Rumored plots included drugging the Gates High football team. According to the gossip, Byzantine High School's team acquired performance-reducing drugs and recruited Gates High students to spy for them. They then smuggled the goods to their planted spies, who would sneak them into Joel Boudin's food, along with the rest of the Gates High School football team. Unsurprisingly, anyone the *Gates Times* directly accused of this would be an enemy of the In Crowd for life.

Sometimes the newspaper only hinted at it for some people, and then made the official accusation the following issue. Eventually those who were hinted at would flock to the *Gates Times* office after school and beg for a chance to be interviewed. If Shelly Boudin was in a lenient mood, they got a chance to explain themselves, disavow Byzantine High School spies and pledge to defend Hallie Flynn against toxic people trying to shame her. Once they did this, there was a significantly smaller chance they would be named as a Byzantine spy in the future.

Shelly published a long message from the editor above the gossip column section where she shared her thoughts.

> Don't listen to Out Crowders. The bulk of the student body is filled with people who harass cheerleaders and mock people and things they don't like, for no other reason than their toxic, internalized thirst to be as mean and toxic as possible.

The article just below her message from the editor was titled "Football Fans are Dead at Gates High." As Shelly put it, the mission of the *Gates Times* was not merely to cover every possible rumor, but to counter certain rumors with more productive rumors. This was how the paper eased into its new and evolving leadership role in steering Gates High School gossip.

Chapter 7: The Gates Sentinel

Joel Boudin was twice as ripped as he had been as a junior. His touchdown dances had lengthened. By the close of the last game they were always well over a minute. He marched down the halls day after day in his football uniform, sending intimidating glares left and right. The Out Crowders cowered back in turn. By contrast, he gave nods of approval to those who had stood up for Hallie and contributed to the *Gates Times*.

While the In Crowd ran into further and further road blocks in their ongoing struggle to stop the toxicity in school from spreading and contaminating GHS with more toxic elements, the *Gates Times* continued to turn up the volume. Gossip columns became even wilder than they had been in the past. Underclassmen reporters began writing guides for how to recognize toxic people, how to avoid toxicity in the age of rampant toxicity and how to avoid becoming toxic yourself. Meanwhile, the gossip columns began speculating more and more on who might be toxic in the school and gave a list of bullet points for each person in question, explaining what the possible indicators of toxic behavior might be.

Tyler Base, a senior who did not have a taste for the gossip columns Shelly Boudin published in her newspaper, decided to take matters into his own hands. He started his own school newspaper, the *Gates Sentinel*. Ms. Eden, the English teacher, became their faculty advisor. As the founding Editor-in-Chief, Tyler got to work organizing the necessary logistics. One day while he was in the gym lockers, he came across a costume for an old, forgotten school mascot from several years back at Gates High: Teddy the Toad. He put the face of Teddy in the top banner of the template for *Gates Sentinel* issues, in roughly the same position as the GHS logo appeared in all issues of the *Gates Times*.

Curious, Isaiah visited the *Gates Sentinel* after school. Even though they had not published an issue yet, the meeting room was already crowded. Numerous former smokers and disgruntled football fans filled the space from wall to wall. With difficulty, Isaiah managed to squeeze himself through and approached Tyler at his desk.

"Hey Isaiah," Tyler greeted, pulling his fellow 12th Grader into a bro-hug. "I haven't seen you since P.E. last year. How have you been?" Beside Tyler was a slender junior girl with pink hair and a polka-dotted shirt. She stood out like a character from the former *Gates Times* funnies.

"Alright," said Isaiah.

"What brings you here?"

"The *Gates Times* is absurd these days. It seems so different this year. I've been reading it for three years and never had a problem with it."

Tyler nodded. "Neither did I. It's the only school newspaper we've ever known, but you're not alone Isaiah. Pretty much everyone I talk to has a nagging feeling inside their head that's something is off about our school now."

"Right," Isaiah concurred. "I heard you were starting a new school paper and wanted to check it out."

"Awesome man," said Tyler. "We need all the help we can get. This here is Marian Jay, Deputy Editor and pop culture columnist."

"Great." Isaiah shook hands with Marian and was now eager to get involved. "So you won't be doing gossip columns like the *Gates Times*, then?"

Tyler shook his head. "The *Sentinel* will have gossip columns alright," he said, his lip curling.

"Oh," said Isaiah, his smile fading. "I thought you were trying to be different."

"And so we will be," said Tyler. "We'll have rival gossip columns and we'll put a check on the *Gates Times*."

"I don't know about that."

"You're a very fine person, Isaiah," said Tyler. "I get why you might have some reservations, but trust me on this for now. Just wait and see."

Isaiah was still unsure of himself. "Well...it does sound different. I guess."

"What would you like to write?" Marian asked Isaiah as Tyler beckoned others in the crowd to come forward.

"I don't know," said Isaiah. "Not gossip columns, though."

"No worries," Tyler interjected. "We need much more than those to fill up a paper."

"Let's find something else then," said Marian Jay. She took out a notepad and pen. "What are your interests?"

"Ummm...I don't know." So far this year Isaiah had been so focused on doing prep work for the Jefferson Lee Scholarship Fund that he hadn't had time for much else.

"I see," Marian Jay sighed. "Do you play any sports or participate in any clubs?"

"Not really," he replied. "I ran track freshman year, but I'm really no expert on sports." Actually, he had spent a lot of his free time hanging out and watching football with Craig and Everett. But the *Gates Times* already covered the football games and if Isaiah was going to write something he didn't want it to be about Joel Boudin and Hallie Flynn.

Marian shrugged. "Perhaps you could write a fitness column for us."

"That's a good idea," Tyler Base said, turning back to Isaiah and Marian Jay. "The *Gates Sentinel* caters to all Gates High Schoolers, so motivational articles are in high demand."

"It has been a few years, Isaiah said, "but I remember some of the coach's tips about keeping in shape."

"That'll do," said Tyler. "Listen, a lot of kids here are lost and don't know what to do with themselves, especially the freshmen. We are in high school, after all. However, the *Gates Times* really isn't helping anybody find themselves."

Isaiah raised an eyebrow. "And the *Gates Sentinel* can?"

Tyler shrugged. "We might as well try."

Isaiah pondered this for a moment. "Fine, Tyler. Sign me up."

As Isaiah left, Tyler and Marian spoke to Yazidi, the new girl. Yazidi resubmitted her article that the *Gates Times* neglected to publish to the *Gates Sentinel*. Tyler told her he was happy to publish her article on her experiences during the War in Yemen and her subsequent coming to America.

The Gates Sentinel; Volume 1, Issue 1

From the Editor: Sentinel's First Issue

Welcome to the first ever issue of our
Gates High's new school publication. My
staff and I decided to start this newspaper
for a key purpose. High school is a criti-
cal time of our life, whether we realize it
now or not. These are the years where we
develop into the men and women we'll be
for years to come, so it's important to focus
on what will better ourselves. From the
so-called "toxic" rumors and all the rabid
gossip written elsewhere, you might think
we live in a pretty barbaric and ruthless
environment. This is not the case at all.
Life at Gates High can still be pretty good
if you subtract all the noise in the background and follow your dreams. Picture
what you want in your head. Overcome
any obstacles. Above all, never apologize
for who you are. I've written an article
myself on the power of positive thinking.
It's on page 2 and 3 if you're interested. I
hope you enjoy all our content. Have an
awesome day.

Tyler Base, Editor-in-Chief

The inaugural issue of the *Gates Sentinel* received much
curious attention. One of its main sections was dedicated to
articles on fitness, staying in shape and general self-help topics
for teens. This section also featured pieces on health, motivation,
losing weight and even dating advice.

The staff of the *Gates Sentinel* was both diverse and all similar at once. Marian Jay became the go-to pop culture columnist for the *Sentinel*. Since the *Gates Times* had nixed their funnies section, the *Gates Sentinel* started their own. The comics all featured Teddy the Toad as the main character.

The *Gates Sentinel* also had certain articles similar to those of the *Gates Times*, such as reviews of the school production of Hamlet. While the *Gates Times* only ever ran positive reviews of the show and Jimmy Hugo's performance as such, the *Gates Sentinel* featured three separate reviews of the show: one positive, one negative and one neutral. Marian Jay wrote the negative review, but mentioned at the end that the author of the positive review was her best friend.

The section that stood out most in the *Gates Sentinel* was the one with the rival gossip columns. Unlike those in the *Gates Times*, these were directed mostly at members of the In Crowd.

Art Teacher in a Coma: The Real Story

There's been a lot of gossip about why we don't have an art teacher. Ms. Monet-Marbleton has yet to make an appearance and the prevailing rumor is that she was in a coma. During our investigation we were able to confirm most of the details of the initial story, but some essential parts were left out. Now the *Gates Sentinel* is here to set the record straight. Yes, Ms. Monet-Marbleton is indeed in a coma, and that coma was caused by a horrific traffic accident. A student at Gates High did cause that traffic accident. The student close to the scene was previously thought to be unidentified. Now we know

that student was none other than Hallie
Flynn, senior and captain of the cheerleading squad.

The "real story" about the art teacher in a coma was beside
another similar *Gates Sentinel* rival gossip column. One of the
second string football players had not been on the field yet this
year due to injury. The gossip column stated that Joel Boudin
shoving second stringer off a two-story balcony back in July
caused the injury.

For a couple days after the *Gates Sentinel* launched, the
Gates Times denied that there even was a second school newspaper at all. They claimed that it was nothing but a conspiracy
rumored about by Byzantine High School spies. Even the most
dedicated readers of the *Gates Times* scoffed at this. There was a
second school newspaper being distributed alongside the first
and that could not avoid being acknowledged for long.

Shelly Boudin, unused to having competition, was dismis-
sive. She stated that the *Gates Times* was the publication with a
history behind its names and everyone sensible knew to come
to it because it was more authentic.

Even though she didn't make it sound like the new publication deserved attention, Shelly did not hesitate to make some
changes with the operations of the *Gates Times*. At first, both
school newspapers shared the stands that the *Gates Times* always
used in the front entranceway. Then the *Gates Times* stepped up
efforts to make itself more visible. Five freshmen girls in their
cheerleading uniforms stood ready to greet students coming in
the early morning and handed out copies of the *Gates Times* to
any student who would take one.

Tyler Base was featured in a *Gates Times* gossip column the very next issue. Supposedly, Tyler was a former student from Byzantine High School who moved so he could pretend to be a student at Gates High, sabotage the football team and discredit the established school newspaper. All the seniors had gone to class with Tyler since elementary school, so they knew this to be false. A few of the underclassmen, however, started to believe it. Tyler Base was not intimidated by gossip spread about him. As the *Gates Times* came after him, the amount of students reading the *Gates Sentinel* grew and grew.

* * *

As the *Gates Times* found the toxic elements at Gates High School were multiplying faster than they could address them in their gossip columns, their reporters and editorialists began to publicly brainstorm how the best way to explain the toxicity at school to new students, or more specifically the eighth graders who would be arriving to visit the school in another week or two. Principal Terrence, on the other hand, got a chance to test explaining it to new arrivals before then.

The Stephensons had just moved to town. Mr. Stephenson had just been offered a new position at Flynn Telecommunications and Mrs. Stephenson had phoned ahead to arrange a meeting with Mr. Terrence. They had a son in ninth grade and a daughter in tenth grade, whom they now had to enroll in a new school.

Mr. Stephenson asked about Gates High, and Principal Terrence gave him a full account of the events of the school year: the break-up blog post, Hallie's Splat, the gossiping of the smokers, the gossip columns of the *Gates Times*, and how all the students were learning about the dangers of toxicity first-hand. Mr. Stephenson had a hard time keeping up. Mrs. Stephenson asked what the school had done about it. Principal Terrence showed them both a copy of the *Gates Times* and explained how the school paper under Editor Shelly Boudin had rallied to Hallie's side.

"We have a student body that helps each other out whenever trouble arises," Mr. Terrence assured.

Soon after the meeting, the Stephensons elected to send their children to a nearby private school.

By this time, word had spread throughout town of what the unusual social scene was at Gates High School. Since many doubted that the school administration was handling it properly, some of the parents and teachers suggested that the superintendent intervene in the situation. However, the mayor forbade the superintendent from getting involved in the "toxic conflict," stating that it was a private matter for GHS to handle on its own without outside involvement. He reached this decision after consulting several individuals with knowledge of what was going on at the high school, including Mr. Flynn.

Of course, that did not prevent uproar at the PTA meeting. The parents of those targeted in the gossip columns were furious. Principal Terrence tried to reassure them. He told them all that the "rumors" in the *Gates Times* were not ordinary schoolyard gossip kids sometimes say behind each other's backs. The gossip columns were researched and written by the staff, published in the Gates High school newspaper underneath the official school logo and distributed to the student body accordingly. Terrence's efforts did nothing to calm the parents down. Quite the opposite in fact.

The biggest anger was over the gossip columns which turned out not to be true. The *Gates Times* promptly took steps to rectify the error. Whenever a gossip column was definitively proven false, the journalist would write a retraction note on the back page. The newspaper was generally full, so these notes were listed together in a corner and in smaller font. Now everyone would know which pieces of gossip turned out to be false, as long as they carried a magnifying glass.

Hallie's father, who had always been too engaged with his business to attend, was now at every PTA meeting. He worked the room and spoke to as many of the other parents as possible prior to the call to order. Since he employed nearly half the town, he knew many of them well already.

Some of the loudest voices in the room asked why the administration didn't seem to be doing anything. Those looking from the outside into Gates High School brought up several concerns. Some parents called Hallie's centralization of gossip in the *Gates Times* counterproductive. Some actually thought the members of the In Crowd were behaving toxic themselves. Most were confused about what qualified as toxic and what did not, since the definition of the word seemed constantly in motion. Mr. Flynn was prepared to address these concerns put forth by other parents, by any means necessary.

Chapter 8: Speech from the Field

On Thursday, Gates High School faced off against Kensington High School in another home game. Kensington was the closest school to Gates in Western County, besides Northern Central High School, so the Kensington players headed to Gates right after school. The students at Gates found their football field had extra bleachers lining it and there was even a cameraman filming. The field had also been neatly trimmed. All other team practices and club meetings were cancelled for the day so that everyone could attend. One of the *Gates Times* gossip columnists had written that she had heard from a friend of an acquaintance of a friend that some kids were planning a "toxic boycott" of the football game, and Hallie persuaded the principal that was something to be avoided.

When the "toxic boycott" rumor broke, Hallie complained to Joel, Joel complained to the coach and finally the coach complained to the principal. In order to prevent any boycotts, a new school policy was enacted to make attendance at football games mandatory.

"Of course, sometimes life gets in the way," Principal Terrence reassured everyone in the morning announcements. "We understand that." Simply being sick, however, was not a valid excuse for missing a football game; even if was for missing ordinary school days. Only a valid doctor's note from a hospital emergency room could excuse a student from attendance on grounds of health.

"Kids might be faking," Hallie asserted.

The penalty for missing a football game was losing credit for a semester. Even if there were kids at school who hated Hallie that much, they would be less likely to stay home from football with such a strong consequence on the table.

Most of the dedicated football watchers at Gates simply shrugged it off. They would have gone to the games anyway, but some felt it would be less fun now that they had to go.

Shelly Boudin addressed the controversy in an editor's note from the *Gates Times*. "Hallie was the one who discovered this crisis to begin with," she wrote. "We should all listen to her experience on how best to proceed. Don't forget that the emerging epidemic of toxic boycotts is merely a small part of the toxic problem at school as a whole."

Despite Shelly's setting the record straight, resentment continued to hang in the air. "Well at least we can still watch the college and professional games in the cafeteria," one sophomore told his friends as they passed by a huddle of football players and cheerleaders in the hall.

Hallie's father had made a generous donation to enable the school to make the new improvements on the football watching experience. The school matched the amount he gave. This forced GHS to delay replacing the ancient school computers and put off hiring a few new substitute teachers in order to set aside the necessary amount. With the football renovations drawing attention, hardly anyone noticed the televisions in the school cafeteria being taken down.

Football Team Suffers Toxic Boycotts

Fans are now ruining the experiences of football and cheerleading. There ought to be a rule against being toxic. While not all Out Crowders are toxic, it is the In Crowd who has taken on the responsibility of policing the school for everyone. Toxic ex-fans of the school football team are now actively organizing boycotts of the games. Clearly, if you're not attending the Gates High School football games, you're being toxic. Some non-patrons try to invoke privileged excuses like "being sick," "being busy" or even "not liking football." From now on it's up to everyone to call out toxicity wherever it lurks. Joel Boudin won't stand for toxicity. The cheerleaders won't stand for it. Neither will we. As a news outlet, we are ordinarily expected to be neutral in our reporting, but that's just not something we can do this time. We're not neutral to the point of being absurd. The *Gates Times* stands with Hallie Flynn.

Summer was long gone and the weather was much colder. Joel Boudin's touchdown dances seemed twice as long as before. Hallie Flynn was remarkably undisturbed. Indeed, she seemed just as comfortable as ever in her petite cheerleading outfit. Veronica Morgan, Joel's freshman girlfriend, wore his team jacket whenever he wasn't using it. She had to roll up the sleeves so that her arms would fit all the way through them.

When everyone was settled in and both of the teams were finished warming up, Coach Ericks approached the center of the field and made an announcement. "Thank you everyone for coming today," he opened. "Good of you all to be here. If I can get everyone's attention for a moment, we have a special treat today. Peter Bach traveled across the state to come to our game," Ericks added, pointing to a little boy standing near to him. "Peter is ten years old and a gifted singer, who is said to have one of the best voices of anyone his age in the entire state. He's also had a rough time growing up, losing both his father and his elder brother to street crime. Peter spent his summer giving numerous concerts across Western County, the proceeds of which go to combating gang violence. If you'd all give him a welcoming round of applause, Peter will now sing the national anthem for us."

Coach Ericks handed the young boy the microphone he had been using. But just as Peter opened his mouth, the microphone was snatched out of his hands once again.

Joel Boudin had marched over and seized the microphone for himself. "Sorry for the mix up, Coach," Joel told Ericks, who was bewildered. "We've got something else planned today instead of the national anthem. Boys and girls, if you'll join me."

Every member of the football team and every cheerleader gathered around Joel, who still had the microphone. Jimmy Hugo from the theater program was down there as well, though no one could remember seeing him walk onto the field.

"What does it take to get so many popular kids together at one time?" Joel asked rhetorically, to the audience of fans.

"Ummm…isn't that every football game?" Isaiah whispered aside to Everett.

"Quiet," said Everett. "I want to hear what they're saying."

"That's right," said Hallie. "So, so many popular kids. I mean, just look at all of us here now. It's quite amazing, isn't it?"

"Think of what all of this must mean!" exclaimed Jimmy Hugo. Isaiah got the impression that Jimmy was very irked this afternoon. The *Gates Sentinel* had just written a rival gossip column alleging that Jimmy lip synced most of his lines because his regular voice was too tepid.

The rest of the football players and cheerleaders all took turns with the microphone saying a line and passing it to the football player or cheerleader next to them.

"So many popular kids gathered here."

"You're about to hear from all of us at once."

"Listen up."

"This is the most important thing you'll hear all day."

"There are some very mean and deplorable people making fun of Hallie."

"People are saying cruel and toxic things about her."

"Because she's pretty."

Hallie herself took the microphone again. "They're just jealous of my Splat move."

"They wish they'd thought of it first," said the junior cheerleader who was next in line.

"We do not think it's cool," said the sophomore football player next to her.

"We're not laughing."

"It is not cool."

"It is toxic."

"Toxic people trapped in their toxic mindsets with all their toxicity."

"And toxic behavior."

Next was a freshman football player who paused and scratched his head. "What was my line again?" When nothing but awkward silence followed, he spoke up again. "Ummm... toxic, toxic, toxic!"

"Toxic people spreading toxicity and lies."

"Toxic, toxic lies."

"Deplorable!"

"Resist toxicity."

"I don't think they even go to Gates. They must be Byzantine High School spies."

"Spies, yes, that's it. Anyone who makes fun of Hallie is a spy from Byzantine High School."

"We don't call anybody names," said Hallie. "These toxic people are just...awful."

"I'm with Hallie," said the football player who came next. "And we are the resisters."

When it was finally done, Coach Ericks managed to get the microphone back once again. "Well, that was interesting," he said. "Time for kick off."

Gates' game against Kensington High School went on longer than a football game normally would. Joel did a five-minute touchdown dance every time that Gates scored a touchdown, whether he was involved or not. His dance lengthened the game time considerably. Hallie's halftime dance she had prepared with the other cheerleaders dragged on as well. The audience sent a chorus of hisses and boos their way, but Hallie and Joel both ignored them consistently. Gates emerged barely victorious with fourteen points to thirteen. Joel Boudin urged Coach Ericks to go return to the field after the game ended. Before everyone went home, Ericks took the microphone one more time so that he could scold "whoever the toxic people in the audience were."

* * *

Every year the *Gates Times* did a short interview to each of the superlative winner at GHS, but this year they forgot to include the winners of Class Clown. In the following days, Shelly left a note in the retraction section stating that this was done "in error." While the *Gates Times* apologized for the mistake, they did not correct it in any subsequent issue.

The *Gates Sentinel* seized upon this opportunity and published – not merely a few chosen quotes like the *Gates Times* did for each of the superlatives – but a full interview of Greg Goldstein by Tyler Base himself.

The Gates Sentinel; Volume 1, Issue 7
Interview with Greg Goldstein

Tyler Base: How are you today, Greg?

Greg Goldstein: I'm doing great, Tyler. Thanks for doing this interview with me.

Tyler Base: You're welcome.

Greg Goldstein: I'd also like to thank all my fellow classmates for electing me Class

Clown. It's humbling to be given such a superlative.

Tyler Base: Hah, you're so modest Greg. I don't think your victory was ever in doubt for most of us.

Greg Goldstein: You flatter me.

Tyler Base: I wanted to ask you something about humor, since you're an expert and all. You know, some people these days say jokes can be toxic. That comes up a lot in the dialogue at Gates High now. Do you agree? Can a joke be toxic?

Greg Goldstein: No. Sometimes they can go too far, but mostly if someone jokes about you, it's stupid to take it personally.

Tyler Base: The "anti-toxic" movement was started this year, mostly to call out bad jokes and hurtful gossip. Let me ask, what do you think of this new movement? Is it helping at all? Are they making progress?

Greg Goldstein: Well, that's a complicated question. Of course people go too far sometimes, but that's to be expected. I mean, we are teenagers. The goal of trying to avoid being toxic is noble, but a lot of the people calling out toxicity seem to be biased in how they go about it. To be honest I'm not really sure the anti-toxic people are doing anything helpful at all. I hope I'm not branded as toxic myself just for saying so.

Tyler Base: There's no need to be ashamed, Greg. I know exactly how you feel. So what do you do when someone goes too far with a joke?

Greg Goldstein: Just don't laugh at it. Definitely don't draw more attention to it. You're only making it stronger. Certain kids here have been doing that way too much. It's made things more awkward for them and it's made things way, way more awkward for the rest of us.

Tyler Base: You sound like you're talking about someone specific.

Greg Goldstein: I won't name names, but it's no coincidence that one or two minor incidents have blown up enough to consume our entire senior year so far. Listen, underneath all this noise, most people have more in common than they might think, In Crowd, Out Crowd, whoever. We're all just teenagers and high school is no place to take ourselves too seriously. This used to be common sense, but clearly we've lost track of that.

Tyler Base: Do you remember when certain things written about over the summer? Conflicts of interest, they called it.

Greg Goldstein: Yeah, that was on a certain blog post written about a certain person. What about it?

Tyler Base: Well, we never really found out what those conflicts were. Frankly, nobody cared, but given everything else that's happened this year, maybe we should look into them. That'll be in an upcoming issue of

the *Gates Sentinel*. Now, let's talk some
about where you get your sense of humor.

Greg Goldstein: Sure Tyler. Fire away.

Tyler and Greg discussed the state of the school, as the
interview took place on the same day that the *Gates Times* published an article titled "The End of Gates High As We Know It"
bemoaning what the school had become. Greg cracked a few
witty lines throughout the article. Kids laughed more at the
Sentinel interview than they ever had at even the funnies section
in the *Gates Times*.

Speaking of funnies sections, the funnies of the *Gates
Sentinel* featured a few comics with Greg being drawn in himself with Teddy the Toad. Under normal circumstances, it was
forbidden for a school newspaper to draw pictures depicting real
individual students in their comics, but Greg had given his written permission to the *Sentinel* just before the issue was released.

Gossip cycles continued. The *Gates Times* published an
article on an alleged underground gambling ring that had existed
below the surface for years. The *Gates Sentinel* published an editor's note highlighting "Ethics in School Reporting." Tyler Base
wrote his own gossip column about the underground gambling
ring article from the *Gates Times*. "'Where can I find it?' I asked
the reporter who wrote that article after I tracked him down,"
Tyler explained. "'I want to know!' But he told me to buzz off.'"

Chapter 9: Do-Over

An unexpected announcement came the next Monday morning. Class Clown was to be voted on again. Earlier in the week, the *Gates Times* had received an anonymous tip for one of its gossip columns that some of the superlatives votes were cast unfairly, and that all of these votes happened to fall in the Class Clown election.

The Gates Times; Volume 69, Issue 20

From the Editor: Class Clown to Be Voted on Again?

Gates High School administration received an anonymous complaint the other day regarding the superlative votes. Although the voting for all of the superlatives has taken place and the final results certified, a number of students have voiced their concern that the vote for Class Clown did not turn out the way they wanted. Hallie Flynn, senior and cheerleading captain, spoke to her father, a concerned Gates High parent, who in turn echoed his own concern to the school. Principal Terrence took all the concerns of those supporting the complaint into consideration, and eventually announced that Class Clown would have a re-vote.

The Yearbook Club faces a tough list of deadlines and their advisor and their student president both want to get the superlative section finalized for eventual production. Initially they were very reluctant to hold off any longer, as they still have the rest of the yearbook to get to. At the end, their cooperation was secured following some behind-the-scenes discussion. It is the sincere wish of the *Gates Times* that any mistakes from the first time around will be handled and that the result of the re-vote will be good for the school.

Shelly Boudin, Editor-in-Chief

Everyone now knew there was a push for a re-vote, even if they had no idea where the push was coming from. The *Gates Times* told them there was a push, though they weren't specific as to who was doing the pushing. The In Crowd also told the Out Crowd that there was a push, though no one was visibly involved in it.

The *Gates Sentinel*, on the other hand, condemned the announcement and accused the pushers of circumventing the normal rules and process.

The Gates Sentinel; Volume 1, Issue 9

From the Editor: Who Are the "Anonymous Complainers?"

Running a school newspaper was something I never even considered until this year. It's been an enlightening experience working with my staff, preparing my own articles and interviewing dozens of students I hadn't talked to before. Until the most recent issue of the *Gates Times* I never once heard anyone say they contested the result of the first Class Clown vote. But now some apparent "anonymous complainers" are pushing to undo a choice we all made together as a school.

This is not how voting is supposed to work. Any concern over who should win or who shouldn't needs to be voiced before the voting takes place. When the voting does take place, we all pick a winner together. Once that's settled, everyone in the school community must accept whatever the results are. Period. It's ironic that those publicizing the announcement are also those who claim to be doing everything in their power to make our atmosphere less "toxic." If anything, this action will only make it more toxic.

Class Clown has already been decided. Let's all move on.

Tyler Base, Editor-in-Chief

The *Gates Sentinel* was continued running gossip columns speculating who was behind the "push" for a re-vote while the *Gates Times* soon moved on to writing gossip columns on who booed at the Kensington football game, and what drove them to be so toxic. Even as they shifted their focus to other topics, Shelly took the time to respond to Tyler's response.

> It appears that a certain classmate of mine who claims to be in a position equivalent to my own is ignorant of the validity of our concerns. He is setting a bad example for Gates High, especially those who read his pile of drivel. Furthermore, he is demanding to know who is advocating for a fresh, fair and inclusive election. It's clear he merely aims to maliciously deny the candidates who came up short a second chance.

> Suppose we complied with his request and made the identity of the pushers public. What would happen then? At the *Gates Times* we are above retaliating against those we disagree with. But what would the readers of the *Gates Sentinel* do if they found out who filed the anonymous complaint? Given the toxicity they pump out to undermine us on a daily basis, it would be sheer idiocy to trust them. Well, their bullying will not work. I am making it my personal responsibility to protect the identity of those making us re-vote.

> Unlike our competitor, we represent anti-toxicity. We do not call people names. Anyone seriously objecting to a re-vote on Class Clown is either being willfully toxic or is a spy for Byzantine High School. Or even both. Toxic Byzantine spies!

Tyler responded to Shelly again.

> My staff and I are talking openly. We're
> trying to have an open conversation as a
> school. We're not hiding from anyone. Let's
> not be elementary schoolers about this and
> devolve into hurling accusations. As fun
> as people may find it to gossip, it gets out
> of hand pretty quickly. It would be best if
> both newspapers tune down the gossip
> columns and return to civil, reasonable
> discourse. I'm not saying I've always been
> perfect in the past, either.
>
> Gossip comes in many forms, but it always
> starts and ends up the same. Some boy or
> girl says or does something. A quote gets
> taken out of context. A misleading pic-
> ture is magnified before the masses. Before
> anybody can put two and two together,
> someone has his or her social life ruined.
> If we seriously want to avoid being toxic,
> we need to avoid steering mobs against
> one another. That is the very definition of
> toxicity. Like I said before, I haven't always
> been perfect, but gossip always begets
> more gossip, and Shelly Boudin should
> have thought her actions through ahead
> of time.
>
> After all, who knows which gossiper is right
> when one gossiper gossips about another
> gossiper? But remember, some gossipers
> must be protected at all costs and some
> gossipers get to have their voice put on a
> pedestal. Gossip is bad, but we need to give

> gossipers the benefit of the doubt sometimes. It's a rule, but not for anyone toxic that says that certain gossip is false. Gossip against such an obviously toxic person who does this is actually good. How did we find out that this gossiper of toxic gossip was toxic? Why, through gossip of course. Kids, remember, toxic is bad, gossip is bad and now gossip is more out of control than ever. That is why I feel the need to gossip.

Tyler Base's last paragraph confused a lot of people. A few fans of the *Gates Sentinel* were dedicated enough to read it through multiple times, and most of those who did found at least one thing they concurred with after doing so.

"How can we vote on Class Clown again?" Isaiah said at lunch. He was categorically baffled by the re-vote announcement. "We already voted on it."

"Beats me," said Craig. "Also, it's just Class Clown. We aren't voting on any of the other superlatives."

"I think they want to get it decided soon," said Everett. "All of the superlatives need to be decided before they can start printing the yearbooks, and I stopped by the Yearbook Club the other day. They're behind schedule already and can't afford to waste any more time."

"It was already decided," said Isaiah. He was surprised how irritated he was getting over a picture in back of the yearbook that didn't really mean anything to most people. "If they're behind then they should just start printing."

"Don't you see, Isaiah?" asked Everett, who was beginning to seem frustrated himself. "They can't. Not until we know the votes were counted fairly."

"This isn't right," said Isaiah. "All the votes were counted the same way, but only Class Clown is getting a do-over. That proves this is just somebody being a petty sore loser. I don't know if it's Marcus O'Reilly or not, but maybe someone else is taking his loss personally. It could be someone else in the In Crowd, or maybe not. I think I'll go to the Yearbook Club after school myself and do an interview with them myself."

Everett gawked at him. "Are you that much of a hypocrite Isaiah? I thought you said you weren't going to write gossip columns."

"This isn't a gossip column," Isaiah corrected him. "I'll ask the Yearbook Club for an interview and I'll only say who's behind the re-vote if I get to the bottom of it. Facts only."

"Sounds like a gossip column to me," said Everett. "I thought you only wrote about staying in shape and all that crap. You're not being very nice."

Craig decided he had had enough before Isaiah had a chance to respond. "Guys, stop it. So you both write for separate newspapers. It's nothing to make a big deal over, and neither is Class Clown, honestly. Let's talk about something else."

* * *

The re-vote happened to take place on the same day that Gates High School received visitors from nearby middle schools. Half a dozen buses filled with eighth graders pulled into the GHS parking lot. Since they would be going to Gates themselves next year, this was their chance to visit and get a pre-orientation of what to expect once they entered high school. Every eighth grader had to buddy up with a student who was already attending Gates High School to be their shadow for the day. Both school newspapers ran articles covering the visit.

Principal Terrence had to rely on current high school students to volunteer to have an eighth grader shadowed with them, and not every kid was jumping at the opportunity to do so. It meant a constant burden to them throughout their regular school day. The eighth graders, meanwhile, were disinterested. They had no schoolwork of their own while they were on their tour of Gates High School, and they wouldn't be attending for nearly a year so there was no pressing need to take everything in.

"I must say I feel kind of sorry for the incoming freshmen," Isaiah remarked at lunch to Craig, Everett and Karen.

"Right," said Craig. "They have no idea what they're getting into. So much has changed this year."

"They take up a lot of space in the classrooms," Isaiah added. He had not agreed to shadow an eighth grader himself, but there were a few kids in his biology class who did. It was the most crowded he had ever seen it.

Karen raised an eyebrow. "Do you have a problem with eighth graders, Isaiah?"

"Not personally, no," Isaiah replied. "It's just-"

"We all used to be eighth graders ourselves, you know," Karen interrupted without letting him finish. "Yourself included, unless you skipped a grade and didn't tell anyone."

"They all had lollipops, too," said Isaiah. Food was forbidden in most classrooms, especially science ones. "Mr. Dyson let them keep them. He said they weren't aware of the rule and didn't see it as a big deal."

"Boo-hoo," said Karen. "Besides, that's not a rule at their school. We can't tell them they can't eat candy here. That wouldn't be fair."

"Isn't the point of this field trip for them to get used to how we do things here?" said Isaiah.

"What is the In Crowd saying to the eighth graders?" Everett wondered aloud. "I hope they're warning them about the toxic environment that they're heading into. A lot of people at Gates aren't very nice and they ought to know that."

"Who knows?" said Craig. "I just can't wait to graduate with all the nonsense going on now."

"I *did* see both Hallie and Joel approaching the eighth graders in the parking lot just as they got off the bus," said Karen. "They were giving them all lollipops out of a giant bowl. That was nice of them."

Craig changed the subject. "So do any of you know when they're announcing the results of the re-vote?" The teachers had conducted the second Class Clown election a little differently than the first one. Instead of having the students cast their ballots while they were in homeroom, they held all the voting in the principal's office and called one homeroom in at a time.

"No idea," said Isaiah, taking a full bite out of his lunch. "I just hope they get on with it already."

* * *

Hallie was in a bad mood.

Kids were finally tiring of sitting with the In Crowd for a day. Not as many were willing to get perks for favors as had initially. If Hallie was going to continue to educate the Out Crowd on the dangers of toxicity, she needed a new approach.

Hallie Flynn went to Coach Ericks' office after school. "Have a seat," the coach told Hallie, gesturing to the empty chair in front of his desk. "What can I do for you?"

"I wanted to continue the discussion which we were having this afternoon," Hallie said simply.

"I see," said Coach Ericks. "Right…I'm sorry Hallie, but I really don't think that this is possible."

"But think how it will help the team," said Hallie. "Don't you want Gates to win all its upcoming games?"

"Of course," said Coach Ericks. "We are all obligated to follow the rules of competition, though, and this would certainly be breaking them."

"Joel didn't think there would be an issue with it."

"Really?" said Coach Ericks, skeptical. "The last time I spoke with him he seemed confident we were going to make the Western County finals again, and he made no mention of this."

"Our game against Kensington was one we only won by one point," Hallie reminded him. "Last year we beat them by twenty-one points. Face it, we need some more muscle if we're going to keep up our winning streak."

"Look," said Coach Ericks. "I know that Antenor, T-Bone and Farouk were all great linemen for us last year, but we can't let them back on the team this season. Gates High School policy clearly states that all student athletes must maintain a B average in order to compete. They're failing all their classes."

"Isn't there a way around that?"

"No there isn't," said Coach Ericks. He was starting to lose his patience. "That is not an exaggeration, Hallie. That is not a figure of speech. They are literally flunking every single course they are enrolled in, except for T-Bone. T-Bone doesn't even show up enough, so he's got all incompletes. Antenor has straight Fs and Farouk also has straight Fs."

"Come on, Coach Ericks," said Hallie. "I need some muscle. I mean, we do. We need some *muscle*. We all do, if we're going to win."

"I appreciate your concern," said the coach. "But I also get the feeling you have some other motive for this."

"What would that be?" said Hallie, acting offended. "All I want is what's best for the team, and the school. So does my dad, as you undoubtedly know. Your nephew just applied to Flynn Communications, didn't he?"

Coach Ericks let out a deep sigh. "Look, I will relay your message to Principal Terrence, but I wouldn't expect much from it."

"Thank you," said Hallie. "That's all I ask for now."

Antenor, T-Bone and Farouk were anomalies at Gates High. Unlike the other members of the In Crowd, they were scarcely ever seen hanging out with their fellow In Crowders, and no one mentioned them much at parties. In fact, not many of their fellow classmates could remember them much in class. The only times they were seen were when they were playing football on a game day (they weren't seen practicing much either) and in the hallways when they were beating someone up.

Principal Terrence didn't make any sort of public announcement about them, but following the meeting with Hallie they were back on the football team and Farouk's parents had cancelled his upcoming enrollment in military school. The trio spent their school days roaming the halls, chasing *Gates*

Sentinel columnists and anyone who had bad things to say about the In Crowd.

Isaiah could not shake the feeling that had been growing at the back of his mind. He had mocked the stupidity of the *Gates Times* gossip columns at first, but when they first debuted he thought they would just be a passing phenomenon. Now he was more troubled. Even as Out Crowders went to sit at the In Crowd table, the rift between the In Crowd and the Out Crowd was wider than it had been in any of Isaiah's prior three years at Gates High. Spaces that all GHS students had always had in common were eroded. Whether the school environment was really toxic or not, it smelled fishier than it had ever been. This was one thing he never had any difficulty remembering. He would not be able to forget it, even if he tried.

The rumors that hordes of students were Byzantine spies were not widely believed. However, it was also rumored that both school newspapers had a plant working in the other to anticipate what tomorrow's news would bring. The *Gates Times* had a spy in the *Gates Sentinel* and the *Gates Sentinel* reciprocated by sending a spy of their own to the *Gates Times*. Most Gates High Schoolers took these rumors as a given at this point.

Meanwhile, a lot of other students grew concerned with the rampant gossip columns, which had become a regular part of student life at Gates High. Recently GHS had hired yet another new guidance counselor – Guidance Counselor Shrill – which brought the total up to three. No other school in Western County had more than one guidance counselor, and this sharp increase had not escaped peoples' notice. Many of those featured in the gossip columns or complaining about toxicity became the most frequent visitors. The newly hired guidance counselors struggled to keep up with kids' differing definitions of toxicity.

Chapter 10: Shocker

The next day Gates High Schoolers were met with a shocking piece of news. Marcus had beaten Greg in the second vote for Class Clown. It had become no less than the front-page news story in the *Gates Times*. The new Class Clown picture was displayed very largely, with Marcus standing where Greg had stood in the earlier version, arm-in-arm with Phoebe, both of them smiling broadly. Some shrugged off the news of the change and went on about their day. Others however were outraged that the earlier result was overturned, for they did not see anything wrong with the first vote for Class Clown with the rest of all the superlatives.

"I liked the old picture better," said Isaiah.

"Yeah," said Craig. "After all it is Class Clown not Cutest Couple." Even as the October weather grew cooler, Craig wore short sleeves that allowed his entire tree-shaped tattoo. Since his mother had grounded him an entire semester of junior year over his tattoo, Craig wasn't going to cover it up until he had to.

"I know it doesn't matter much but it still kind of annoys me." Even Isaiah never knew how much he apparently cared about something routine and pointless like Class Clown.

"These gossip columns trouble me," Craig said aloud one day. "I thought they were a passing fad which would come and go, but not only have they not gone away, they're more absurd than ever. They just talk about who's being toxic, who to talk to about toxic people and how to avoid toxic people. We're spreading fear of the invisible!"

"Agreed," said Karen. "Besides, with all these wild stories going back and forth between the school newspapers I don't even know what's supposed to be the truth anymore." Karen was deep in thought. "Even if we could figure out what the truth was, are these really the kind of stories we should be spending our time on?"

"People really shouldn't talk about Hallie Flynn behind her back," said Everett. "It's not very nice."

"Is it very nice when anyone talks behind anyone's back?" Isaiah asked Everett, but he didn't get an answer.

Hallie Flynn's hair draped over her backpack and touched her pom-poms as she walked through the hallway. Most cheerleaders at Gates High attached their pom-poms to their backpacks. Unlike the dirty noses, people actually followed this trend of Hallie's. Her great campaign against toxicity had now reached new heights.

Antenor, T-Bone and Farouk roamed around the school beating up students at a rate that far exceeded what they had done in the past. This season they were more or less exclusively going after students who were called "toxic" in the gossip columns of the *Gates Times* (not those featured in *Gates Sentinel* gossip columns). A few students began complaining to the principal about the three of them, but nothing had been done just yet.

"It's no longer just Hallie who's facing toxic problems at this school," wrote a gossip columnist for the *Gates Times*. "After I got a D on my latest English quiz, I shared my woes with everyone.

No one understood. I even got asked why I didn't study if I didn't like my grade. I had to go to the guidance counselor. This toxic environment is just too much for me."

The Gates Times; Volume 69, Issue 22

Guidance Counselors: Who They Are

There are now four guidance counselors at Gates High. Considering nowhere else in Western County has more than one guidance counselor, this is quite a distinction for us. When you hear "guidance counselor" spoken here, everyone immediately thinks of Guidance Counselor Bethany. This is understandable. After all, for many years she was the only one to turn to at GHS. That was until our school environment became too toxic for her to handle all on her own. Now students in need of consultation therapy may also turn to Guidance Counselors Griffin, Shrill or Jones.

Guidance Counselor Griffin's all-time favorite food is lasagna. Guidance Counselor Shrill is an active member of her church. Guidance Counselor Jones is actually a former Gates High School student himself. So, if you're so worn down by toxicity that you need someone to turn to and would feel better if that person is an alumnus who knows our school, he's your guy. In fact, he played football when he attended here and supposedly he was pretty good. He claims that he almost went on to play college football for Big City University. Brett Webster has genuinely achieved that more recently.

These members of our faculty combat toxicity on their own front invisible us most of the time, and all four tell stories of their own struggles in the process. Even Guidance Counselor Bethany, who has been here by far the longest, says she has to keep a notebook on the different forms of toxicity students come to her about and what students consider to be toxic problems. If a student feels the environment around them is "extra-toxic" they may even require the assistance of more than one guidance counselor. In spite of the fact that three only came to Gates this year, all four are now recognizable faces for much of the student body. They also seem to have bonded with one another over their own struggles. Rumor has it that the quartet of them now barhop together every evening after work.

The *Gates Sentinel* also wasn't running low on things to say. Tyler Base followed up on a promise he had made during his interview with Greg Goldstein.

Brett Webster wrote a note, which was posted a blog over the summer. It's been a while, but it mentioned some possible conflict of interest a certain cheerleader may or may not have been involved in. Now is about time to investigate some of those claims. The *Gates*

> *Sentinel* is here to being you the details and
> leave you to draw your own conclusions. It's
> a discussion we need to have as a school with
> all facts and perspectives taken into account.

Teddy the Toad's comics continued to remain popular. He now had a supporting cast of companion characters, including the Crying Kitties. Marian Jay now collaborated on most of Teddy's comics.

The *Gates Times* ran an article titled "This is What a Toxic Person Looks Like", featuring a photo of Roy Wilson. The writer claimed he witnessed Roy stealing the pet iguana from one of the science classrooms. Roy got many dirty looks that day, despite said iguana still being in its tank. The *Gates Sentinel* wrote a response called "This is What a 'Toxic' Person Looks Like" which, unlike the *Gates Times,* interviewed Roy himself and featured a picture of him feeding the iguana while biology teacher Mr. Dyson watched. Ms. Monet-Marbleton stood by Mr. Dyson's side, perfectly healthy. The art teacher had a baby over the summer and was still on maternity leave when the school year started. Now she was back to work.

"I don't understand it," Shelly Boudin vented in her latest message from the editor. "How can those people (the *Gates Sentinel*) sit there, print their articles and act like their viewpoint is as valid as ours?" Her articles and messages from the editor were becoming more vitriolic. "It is inherently violent and toxic to call the certified results of the official re-vote into question," Shelly Boudin went on to say on her regular article within that issue. She made comments about the re-vote similar to the comments Tyler Base made about the original result before the re-vote. "We need the faculty to step up on this so that everyone knows that the re-vote was legitimate."

The rivalry was not confined to words on newspaper pages anymore. Both editorial staffs received threatening notes on a daily basis. The *Gates Times* blamed the *Gates Sentinel* for their threats. The *Gates Sentinel*, meanwhile, called on everyone to stop sending threats to both newspapers.

Chapter 11: Scandal

The *Gates Sentinel* shocked the entirety of Gates High School with their next front-page story.

The Gates Sentinel; Volume 1, Issue 14

Class Clown Re-vote Rigged!

This is breaking gossip of the highest priority. Gates High's second election for Class Clown was rigged by foul play. Senior school newspaper editor Shelly Boudin raised eyebrows by stating anyone who questioned the second vote would be labeled "toxic." On earlier days Shelly herself was the one supporting the questioning of the first superlative vote. Undoubtedly she would have claimed that anyone who pointed out that obvious distinction was toxic as well. As it turns out, Shelly's own fraternal twin brother Joel Boudin was one of those involved.

That's right. This wrongdoing goes all the way up to the top of the In Crowd. Hallie Flynn and Joel Boudin hatched a plot together. They put it into force when the re-vote for the Class Clown superlative coincided on the same day that eighth graders were visiting Gates. On a day when most were too distracted to notice, Hallie and Joel snuck the eighth graders into the principal's office to cast votes for Marcus O'Reilly. They secured the middle schoolers' cooperation by bribing them with candy.

"This all makes sense now," said Isaiah. "It looks like the In Crowd was behind it after all. If this turns out to be true, they're going to have a lot of explaining to do."

"Don't tell me you actually believe what the *Gates Sentinel* is saying at this point," said Everett. "Everything in there is the opposite of what's in the *Gates Times*. You should see how hard we have to work to counter the toxicity of the rival gossip columns. I covered sports for the *Gates Times* last year, but this year Shelly's had me swamped with gossip intelligence to research."

Isaiah let out a deep sigh. "Everett, there had to be a reason why the result was different the second time around."

"Just because it confirms the ridiculous gossip narrative inside your head doesn't make it true," said Everett. "You're only saying it because the *Gates Sentinel* is the one doing the so-called reporting. Face it. The first time everyone voted wrong and the second time everyone voted the way that they were supposed to vote the first time. The other day you actually called other people sore losers, but now the only sore loser is you. Isaiah, you're pathetic."

"Stop putting words in my mouth." Although Isaiah was growing more annoyed by the second, he managed to control his own tone. "Nothing is true just because it comes from the

Gates Sentinel. The same goes for the *Gates Times*. While I haven't seen the evidence with my own eyes, what I've read is pretty compelling. I'll ask Tyler Base about it later. If his evidence is genuine, then we'll know once and for all how despicable the In Crowd are."

"Isaiah, you're completely missing the point," Everett objected. "The question isn't whether or not the In Crowd did what they're accused of. The problem is how shameful it is that the In Crowd is being accused of it. Try to have a little bit of empathy, Isaiah. How would you feel if you were in Hallie Flynn's shoes right now? Or Joel Boudin's? You're not being very nice."

"I stand by what I said before," Isaiah said firmly. "At the end of the day what matters is the truth, Everett." Isaiah turned to his other best friend. "What do you think?"

Craig had quietly sat out the entire argument so far. "I think I wish all these gossip columns and rival gossip columns would just go away and we could all go back to normal," he finally said.

"Agreed," said Everett. "But you have to admit some gossip columns are more toxic than others, right?"

"To be honest I don't really know what to think about this gossip or that gossip," Craig replied. "First of all, I never wanted to spend so much time on superlatives. I guess it's too late for that now that everyone and their boyfriend and their girlfriend and their brother and their sister are talking about it. Everett, I don't buy the idea that calling out is somehow worse than actually doing something." After a few seconds of silence, Craig decided that he had more to say. "I like Isaiah's last idea. Let's wait and see what happens before jumping to conclusions. That's the right thing to do. Otherwise we're all nothing but a bunch of mini-gossip columnists ourselves."

"Fine," said Everett, resigning himself to the situation. "But you guys should be more careful. People may think you're spreading toxic talk just by enabling it."

"Why?" said Isaiah. "Because the In Crowd is perfect?" Still curious about what the In Crowd had to say about the *Gates Sentinel* story, Isaiah turned to glance over at the In Crowd, but he couldn't find any of them in the cafeteria.

The *Gates Times*, however, was swift in their rebuttal. They echoed Everett's viewpoint to the letter.

> Too many of these people talking about what the In Crowd did. That is not the point. Look at how the *Gates Sentinel* is reacting to recent events. That's the real point. If anyone tried to rig the re-vote for Class Clown, it's the *Gates Sentinel*. With multiple school newspapers running gossip, the student body at Gates High has become overwhelmed. Back when the *Gates Times* was the only newspaper on the block, everyone could always rely on us to inform them which gossip is most important. Too many differing viewpoints running around just confuses everybody. You can't trust people to vote correctly under such conditions.

It remained a mystery how the In Crowd themselves would respond to the allegations against them. As a matter of fact, the In Crowd was nowhere to be seen by anyone. The space in the center of the diamond cafeteria was deserted. There was no mass of GHS colors because no one was wearing a football uniform or a cheerleading uniform. Hallie, Joel and all of their teammates were not present.

A pair of underclassmen stood near the empty In Crowd tables clutching full trays of food, looking around in confusion. The two Out Crowders both refrained from sitting down. Sitting in the In Crowd's seats meant nothing if the In Crowders were not present themselves.

"Where is everyone?" said sophomore Gary Jackson. "If they don't show up I'd better be able to come back tomorrow."

"Yeah," said sophomore Anna Mason. "Me too. I just reached my interview quota. I can't have that all be for nothing." Their voices of complaint were not heard. Both invitees had been abandoned by their hosts.

Chapter 12: The Principal's Office

After lunch, Isaiah, Craig and Everett left the cafeteria and started walking in the direction of their next classes. Everett made a remark about how Antenor, T-Bone and Farouk were tracking down those who were questioning the election results. Everett did not sound disturbed when he said so, and Isaiah found that disturbing. While they were walking something else grabbed all of their attention. A very loud chant was coming from the principal's office. The principal's office was usually as quiet as the library. Everett held the door open for Isaiah and Craig as they got ready to satisfy their curiosity.

"Shut it down! Shut it down! Shut it down!" Every football player and cheerleader in the school was there, shouting it in unison. Isaiah, Craig and Everett joined a handful of other members of the Out Crowd coming in to catch a peek of what was going on. A few of them actually joined in with the In Crowd.

Principal Terrence's secretaries stood up to greet the mob at first. Soon, however, they were overwhelmed and returned to sitting at their desks, their eyes wide as marbles, exchanging looks with one another. Principal Terrence himself was nowhere to be found.

Isaiah looked around. "Okay, what's going on here?"

"What's going on is that our latest story seems to have rubbed some people the wrong way." Tyler Base walked up and stood beside Isaiah, appearing quite pleased with himself.

"Is it true?" Everett asked Tyler, sounding somewhat skeptical. "Did they really rig the Class Clown election by giving lollipops to the eighth graders, or is this just another one of your gossip columns?"

"Oh, it's not just gossip this time," said Tyler. "We've got mountains of evidence for it. Listen to how the In Crowd is desperately trying to sweep this one under the rug. This is going to be priceless."

"What do you mean?" Craig asked him.

"Let me put it to you this way. Nobody will be doing them any favors simply to sit with them at lunch anymore. They're finished."

Hallie continued to lead the chants from just in front of the secretaries' desks. "Shut it down! Shut it down!" she continued to lead as much of the portion of the student body gathered there repeated after their leader. "Resist toxicity!" shouted Hallie.

"Resist toxicity!" the rest of the In Crowd repeated.

"Shut down the *Gates Sentinel*!" yelled Hallie.

"Shut down the *Gates Sentinel*!" echoed the rest.

"What's going on guys?" Karen had just entered the room herself. She turned off her cell phone and put it in her backpack. Everything in front of her now had her full attention.

"Chaos," said Everett.

"Total chaos," Craig concurred.

Finally, Principal Terrence opened the door to his office and emerged into the entranceway. "Alright, I'm coming out," he said, exasperated, as the noise filling up the whole room gradually simmered down. "Hello, all you students who have come to my office with no appointment to yell really loudly. What can I do for you?"

Tyler Base was ready. "Mr. Terrence," he spoke up before anyone else could and approached the principal with a clipboard in hand. "On the day of the re-vote for Class Clown, there were about two hundred visiting eighth graders. As you can see, not only did Marcus get about two hundred more votes than he did the first time, but there were two hundred more *total* votes than when all the other superlatives were voted on. There were two hundred more votes for Class Clown in the re-vote than there are students in the school."

"Lies," hissed Shelly Boudin.

"Toxic, toxic lies," screamed Hallie Flynn.

From the back of the crowd, Antenor, T-Bone and Farouk all growled in unison.

"Furthermore," Tyler continued, looking around at all the other kids in the entrance to Principal Terrence's office. "It appears that certain students were giving out pieces of candy to the visiting incomers that day, and that they snuck them into the voting booths between the time when separate homerooms were called. We spoke to kids with brothers and sisters in middle school. In addition, we have dozens of signed and written testimonials to confirm this. I mean, it's not exactly rocket science to see what took place here."

Shelly Boudin was spitting mad by the close of Tyler Base's rant. "Don't listen to him, Mr. Terrence. Tyler is the Editor-in-Chief of the *Gates Sentinel*, and his toxic words are not to be trusted. Did you see the *Sentinel*'s review of the school production of Hamlet? Absolutely disgusting. The Byzantine High Schoolers probably told him to do it."

"So they wrote a negative review of Hamlet," said Principal Terrence. "Everyone is entitled to his or her own opinion of the quality of performance art. I don't see how that's 'toxic', but then again the definition of that word seems to change every day as I hear it used in different contexts. The *Gates Sentinel* also published a positive review of Hamlet alongside that one, if I'm not mistaken."

"That wasn't a real positive review," said Shelly. "They were mocking it. They were mocking everyone. It was toxic."

"Hahaha," Tyler laughed. "Can you just listen to yourself for a minute, Shelly? You can barely even keep up with your own gossip anymore. So a few kids were saying some mean things about a few other kids. That's simply how high school is. The best way to deal with it is not give it any more power than it already has."

"We're far past that point," Shelly told him. "It was needless of you to start a second school newspaper when we already had a perfectly good one."

"If you're so perfect, why are you so afraid of the idea of another school newspaper?" Tyler asked.

Shelly took a deep breath. "Fact check. This isn't just 'a few kids saying some mean things about a few other kids'. This is a toxic, toxic environment caused by you and your gossip columns. It's so toxic. You are toxic, the symbol of true toxicity and all that is wrong and toxic here at Gates."

"Easy, Shelly," said Tyler. "You're supposed to be a writer, so you might want to work on your word variation a little. Just a suggestion." Although the room had still been loud moments earlier, it was now quieter as everyone listened to Tyler and

Shelly's banter. Hardly anyone had ever seen the two of them in the same place at the same time before, despite all their back-and-forth between the *Gates Sentinel* and the *Gates Times*. At last the gossip columns and rival gossip columns had flown off the newspaper pages, manifested and come to life before their eyes. "Fact check. You started your gossip columns first."

From the background, Isaiah glanced aside at Everett, Craig and Karen. He then went back to watching Tyler and Shelly with the rest of the audience. As the two school newspaper editors sparred, Isaiah pondered what he would say if he were a part of the dialogue himself. Bitterness crept through his veins as he held his tongue. Somehow Isaiah felt like it was wrong to restrain himself during the action. On the other hand, since Tyler was already out in the fray, there was no need to put himself out there. He would be risking his reputation if he did. Tyler was winning on his own, so Isaiah risking himself would just be stupid.

"Yeah, Tyler's got this handled," Isaiah mumbled under his breath. Laying low was the right call.

"Huh?" said Karen.

"What did you say Isaiah?" Everett asked him.

"Nothing." Isaiah could not help but wonder, though. If standing back really was the right call, why did something feel so wrong about it?

"Don't you dare compare your gossip columns to ours," Shelly shot back at Tyler, now even madder than she was before. "At the *Gates Times* we practice sophisticated, authentic, approved gossip in all our news stories."

Principal Terrence saw fit to interject. "Approved high school gossip?" he said, as though he did not believe such a thing existed. "Approved by whom?"

Shelly scoffed. "Do I have to explain everything to you, Mr. Terrence?" But she moved right along. "If you have a heart, Tyler, just look at what your gossip columns have done to the school. It's tearing us apart. I miss when we could sit down and have civil discourse."

"Really?" said Tyler. "Because that's something we actually agree on, Shelly. I too wish we could all just go back to normal. You're the Editor-in-Chief of the *Gates Times*. I'm the Editor-in-Chief of the *Gates Sentinel*. Let's steer everything back to civil discourse. You and I can start a whole new trend right here right now. What do you say?"

Shelly was fire truck-red in the face. She had clearly not expected this response. "No, I don't think so," she replied. "As much as I want to have civil discourse back, that won't be possible until we take out all the toxic people like you."

"They are a disgrace," Hallie interjected. "These people are making fun of sitting members of the cheerleading squad and they need to be disciplined!"

At this point Principal Terrence saw fit to interrupt again. "Let's just take a deep breath and take a step back, everyone. I knew these gossip columns were a terrible idea. I told Mrs. Friedman that from the start. Later I told Ms. Eden the same thing. Now, things have gotten way out of hand."

"At the *Gates Sentinel* we have gossip columns," Tyler admitted. "But we use them to broaden the window of dialogue. We just want open discussion."

The principal shook his head. "It ends today."

"No Mr. Terrence," Shelly said, ignoring what Tyler had just stated. "The *Gates Times* started its gossip column as a way to spread awareness about the toxic problems at our school. Everything we've done has been in the service of resisting toxicity."

"That makes absolutely no sense," said the principal.

"Sir," one of the younger football players called out. "Let's stop beating around the bush and get to what this is really about. Whose side are you on? Gates High or Byzantine High?"

Tyler Base rolled his eyes. "Geez, not this again."

"Well I'm the principal of Gates High. What do you think?"

"Evan Terrence is the captain of Byzantine High's football team," said the boy. "You have the same last name. Are you related?"

"No," said the principal. "And it would be none of your business if I was related to him."

"I think you're hiding something," said the boy. The group of cheerleaders behind him all shouted echoes of approval.

The principal picked up an old issue of the *Gates Times* off of one of the secretary's desks. "How exactly does 'Eddy Steals Wheelchair Kid's Lunch, Dangles It Just Outside of Reach Above His Head' educate kids on not being toxic?"

"Simple," said Shelly. "We're showing everyone what being toxic looks like, and pointing out to them who is toxic so they know to stay away from them."

"But even your own article says that this is just rumors and speculation, and no one actually saw it happen," said Principal Terrence. "That's buried three paragraphs beneath the headline. Also, not once in this article do you interview either Eddy or the kid in a wheelchair in question."

"Right," Shelly admitted. "Well, the gossip columns can only speculate on what *may* be true. There's so much toxicity around the school we wouldn't be able to cover it all if we waited on evidence for everything."

"Besides, it's more important to be anti-toxic than to be factually accurate," Hallie added.

"And what about Eddy?" asked Principal Terrence. "Have you considered what you're putting him through?"

"With all due respect Mr. Terrence, I don't think you understand the full extent of the problem," Hallie Flynn said. "Since the beginning of the year and earlier I've experienced all of it first-hand."

"Oh here we go again," Tyler Base muttered under his breath.

"I've suffered pain and humiliation at the hands of toxic football fans every time I step on that football field," said Hallie. "I resist the urge to call it quits, so I wind up subjecting myself to more and more every time I do my service to the school. I can just hear the toxic people whispering to each other from the top of my pyramid. Toxic people mocked me after the break-up blog. Toxic people mocked my Splat move."

"Wow," said Everett. "I can't watch."

"She's losing it," said Isaiah.

"She's making a fool of herself," said Craig. "This could cost her Prom Queen in May."

"By the end of today I don't think she'll even still be cheer-leading captain," said Tyler Base.

"And now, on top of everything else, you force me to listen to this," Hallie said to Principal Terrence. The rest of the room were silent, and even most of the In Crowd were looking away from her, unable to deal with being humiliated alongside one of their leaders. "You deny my experiences and condescend about me being paranoid from your position of privilege."

Joel Boudin tugged at Hallie's shoulder. "Alright, come on," he said. "We've done our best, but I think this is over now."

Hallie jerked her shoulder away from Joel, staying fully focused on the principal. "Your cruelty is only enabling this toxicity to spread further and deeper into our school." She was on the verge of bursting into tears. "I can't believe you," she cried. "If only you would just acknowledge your internal toxicity we could finally end this. You have the power but you refuse to use it."

The principal put up his hand and attempted to get a word in. "Hallie-" he began.

"I'll tell my dad on you!" she snapped, her eyes beginning to water. "You can forget about ever coming to one of his charity fundraisers again." As she finished, Hallie collapsed to her knees, bawling incessantly and dampening the carpet.

Several long moments of tense silence followed. At last, Principal Terrence broke it. "Please forgive my ignorance, Hallie. I had no idea how much this meant to you."

"Wait, what?" Tyler Base said under his breath. "You can't be serious."

Hallie turned her head away from the principal. "With all due respect, Mr. Terrence, those are just words."

"Okay," said Principal Terrence. "I think we've all learned a valuable lesson here, even if it took a while. Shelly Boudin, Tyler Base, no more gossip columns. They bring nothing but trouble."

"Absolutely not," snapped Shelly, now joining Hallie in going back on offense. "Like I explained before, the *Gates Times* gossip columns are essential ammunition in the war against toxicity. There's no validity on *all sides*. It's pretty black and white and straightforward. The *Gates Sentinel* is causing *obstruction* of our trying to end the toxic problem."

"I see," said Principal Terrence, though he still didn't sound like he was quite on the same page as her. "Very well then. I'll concede to your demands and give you what you want. The *Gates Sentinel* is shut down."

Every football player in the room was in pure disbelief, but they soon burst into a team cheer. The cheerleaders hugged one another and cried tears of joy as their captain snatched victory from the jaws of defeat.

Not everyone in the room shared the same sentiment. "You can't shut us down but not the *Gates Times*," yelled Tyler Base. "That's not fair, Mr. Terrence."

"I agree," said Isaiah. He had not been outspoken in the conversation before, but now he couldn't help himself. "In fact, I think that that's unconstitutional."

"Can it, nerd boy!" Joel Boudin shouted across the room at Isaiah. "Stop trying to sound so smart with your big words."

An explosion of laughter filled the entrance to Principal Terrence's office. Every member of the In Crowd carried it from one end of the room to the other, and then back and forth across the room many times. The principal himself, looking uncertain at first, eventually forced a laugh of his own to join in. His secretaries each smiled weakly, and then turned to their computer screens, isolating themselves off from the scene surrounding them.

No sooner had the room quieted down enough that Principal Terrence raised his voice again. "Okay, the show's over," he said. "Everyone get back to class."

The In Crowd wasted no time in leaving his office, now that they had been given what they had asked for. Isaiah, Tyler and some others wondered if their staying put would make a difference, but a pair of security guards arrived in the office at that moment to shoo them out. Students tripped over each others feat, running and skipping out of the office as the security guards struggled to stand straight and direct the traffic out to the hallway in an orderly fashion.

* * *

If anyone believed that Gates High would return to normal following the confrontation in Principal Terrence's office, they did not remain hopeful for long. The War on Toxicity only escalated in the following days. Anyone suspected to be making fun of Hallie or any other member of the In Crowd was immediately cornered. The front page of the *Gates Times* had an enormous picture of the cheerleading captain smiling underneath a giant headline stretching from one side of the newspaper to the other.

Hallie Persisted!

The Anti-Toxic movement at Gates High won a decisive major victory the other day. Hallie and those close to her have changed our school by becoming unlikely leaders in fighting toxicity. What began as an overblown controversy over repeating the Class Clown election has brought more awareness to students' own actions.

"The first time I voted for Greg," said Anna Mason, sophomore. "I also thought overturning the first vote was unfair, but maybe it was the fair thing to do, and maybe I should be ashamed for voting against Marcus before."

But just because Gates High School has learned how to elect a superlative winner correctly does not mean everything is resolved. Readers of the former *Gates Sentinel* continue to lurk everywhere among us. It is up to the In Crowd and Out Crowd alike to root them out and confront their biases one-by-one or this school will stay irreparably toxic.

The *Gates Times* was able to track down a former *Gates Sentinel* reader. He apologized for any hurt he caused by subscribing to such toxic material. This week he will be in detention, but he promised to turn over a new leaf in the future, asking others to confess and seek help as he has. For the time being his identity will remain confidential. Should he revert to toxicity in the future, we at the *Gates Times* will tell on him. Those threatened by our battle against toxicity are unwelcome in our welcoming environment for all.

Naturally, the regular readers of the *Gates Sentinel* were displeased with the new development, and they weren't given any breathing room to digest it. The *Gates Times* was pulling no punches. Shelly's following statement made that clear.

The Gates Times; Volume 69, Issue 27

From the Editor: School Environment Remains Toxic

Despite the comfort I feel at how Principal
Terrence handled recent events, I cannot get
over my solemn feeling. It's truly shameful
that things have gone as far as they have. No
one was happy at the end of that gathering.
I was there. Yes, a great victory was won.
Gates High School is still a very toxic place
and every member of the student body still
has to remain on alert. In the meantime, the
Gates Times will continue the good fight to
eradicate the problem. We must be vigilant.
Our reliable gossip columns will endure
until every last remaining ounce of toxicity
is purged from the school forever.

Shelly Boudin, Editor-in-Chief

As far as the matter of Class Clown went, Marcus O'Reilly
scheduled a meeting with Principal Terrence to discuss the
course of the election. Greg Goldstein assured everyone that he
would go to meet with the principal with Marcus and he would
repeat everything the *Gates Sentinel* recently discovered while
he was there, but Greg was not invited to Marcus' closed-door
meeting with Principal Terrence. Joel Boudin and Hallie Flynn
both were, though nobody could figure out why. After the fif-
teen-minute meeting, the principal announced that the results of
the more re-vote were finalized and that there would be no more
debate about the fairness of the voting procedures.

Principal Terrence also authorized for kids to be given
detention for acting toxic. At Hallie's request, he encouraged
anyone who saw one of their fellow classmates behaving in a toxic
way – major or minor – to report them to Mr. Zee for detention.

This went for not just for toxic actions, but also for toxic words and suspected toxic thoughts.

The In Crowd could only rely on their allies to report toxicity so much, so they continued to have their own enforcers patrol the school. Antenor, T-Bone and Farouk roamed the hallways during the day and beat up anyone they suspected of acting toxic. Many objected to these methods, but those objections were mostly ignored.

Chapter 13: A Bad Day

Isaiah bumped into Tyler Base on his way from Calculus to History. "Hey Isaiah," Tyler greeted. He was not by himself, but was accompanied by two junior boys and one freshman who was tagging along with them. The freshman was at least a head shorter than all the upperclassmen around him and appeared to have one foot in puberty and one foot out.

"Hey Tyler," said Isaiah. "Hey guys," he said to everyone else, since he didn't know their names. "Sorry about the *Gates Sentinel*."

Tyler leaned in and lowered his voice. "The *Gates Sentinel* is still fully-operational. We're not going to let something stupid like getting banned stop the presses."

"I see," said Isaiah. "Won't you get in trouble?"

Tyler smirked. "We're not planning on getting caught, man. And if we are, so we'll get a day's detention. That's not the end of the world." The two junior boys nodded.

"I ain't afraid of no getting detention," said the freshman. His voice cracked in and out as he said this.

Isaiah looked down at the outspoken ninth grader, unsure how to respond. "Ummm…good for you, I guess. But Tyler, how will you even distribute it? I doubt Ms. Eden will want to lose her job defying the principal over this."

"No, Ms. Eden advised us to keep our heads down for now. She says she'll try to convince Terrence to change his mind once things cool down," said Tyler. However, he waved this objection away. "I know she means well, but we don't need her permission to continue publishing."

"I just don't see how it can work," said Isaiah. "You can't use the stands in the lobby if your publication's banned."

Tyler shrugged. "We'll find other ways to get the message out: stuffing them in kid's lockers, passing out copies to our friends in secret, whatever we have to do to get our message out. A few things might go wrong here and there, but fail fast then try again."

"Is this still about the Class Clown election?" asked Isaiah. "Look, I wasn't happy about that either, but you're better off letting that go. At the end of the day, it is just one stupid picture in the yearbook."

"No," said Tyler. "That's in the past now. We lost that battle, but the war continues. So Hallie felt bad because some people talked behind her back. Boo-hoo. Show me one kid in high school that's never happened to. Now she's spreading her anger about it through the entire school in a deranged rampage. It's time we stand up for ourselves and say we won't let her get away with it anymore. We tried everything else and now we need to keep fighting fire with fire. It's the only option left to us."

"Won't she keep fighting back with bigger fire?" asked Isaiah.

"Sure, but what's she going to do? Call us toxic? She's already labeled the entire Out Crowd as toxic. We've just got to get used to being called toxic and not living in fear of people calling us names."

"Maybe," Isaiah admitted.

"There's more to it than that, Isaiah," said Tyler Base. "You see, if we don't take matters into our own hands than someone else will."

Isaiah didn't quite follow. "What do you mean?"

"One of my former rival gossip columnists posted a blog last night on Veronica," said Tyler.

"Joel Boudin's girlfriend?" Isaiah didn't know much about her. She was very quiet.

"Yes," said Tyler. "The blog said she's a kleptomaniac who's addicted to crack. A chain email was sent to half the *Gates Sentinel* staff last night."

"Who wrote the gossip blog?" Isaiah asked.

"I won't dignify the guy by mentioning his name," said Tyler. "From the day he started writing for us something always seemed off about him. Since he was acting on his own, there was nothing I could do. I would have forbid him to write about Veronica in the *Gates Sentinel*."

"Because she's in ninth grade?"

"No," Tyler said, shaking his head. "Because she's a civilian. Veronica has never gossiped about anyone. I've always found her relationship with Joel kind of sketchy. I'd write a gossip column on him about that. Writing a separate gossip column solely about her is just plain wrong."

"Of course it is," said Isaiah. "The *Gates Times* wouldn't hesitate to do something similar, though."

"No, they wouldn't," said Tyler. "They recklessly target whomever they like, but that doesn't mean we should. We have to show we're different."

"Right," said Isaiah. "I completely agree."

"That's why keeping the *Gates Sentinel* afloat underground is so important Isaiah," said Tyler. "We need to show there's a right way and a wrong way to fight back."

"I see."

"We could really use your help, Isaiah," said Tyler. "Your articles weren't the most edgy, but people respected them. Now the *Gates Sentinel* needs all hands on deck if we're going to survive. We are the resistance, Isaiah. The *real* resistance."

Part of Isaiah wanted to say yes. Tyler Base had a magnetic aura, which lay in the simple truth that he genuinely didn't care what people thought. "I don't think so, Tyler. Don't get me wrong. I get what you're doing, but things are getting really ugly and escalated right now and I'm still trying to get accepted into a scholarship program at Big City University. I really need to just lie low for the rest of the school year and try to tune this noise out."

Tyler's three underlings railroaded Isaiah. "Pansy!" said one of the juniors.

"I heard he let Karen cheat on him back when they were dating while he watched," said the second junior. "No wonder she dumped him."

"Pathetic," the first junior spoke again. "You're going in my next gossip column you traitor."

The freshman boy also said something, but not loud enough to be heard above the others. From the way he rolled his eyes Isaiah could guess the nature of it.

"What?" Isaiah said, astonished. "That's not true. Where did that come from? So random."

Tyler held up a hand to calm them down. "Leave him alone boys. He's a good guy. Isaiah, sorry to hear that, man. I hope you reconsider. Why don't you take a copy of today's issue and think it over?"

Isaiah doubted that would make a difference, but allowed for Tyler to discretely slide a copy of the *Gates Sentinel* into his binder before they parted ways. Several feet away Marian Jay was just closing her locker, ever recognizable with her pink hair and polka-dotted shirt. She shook her head at Isaiah, who broke eye contact and strode off the other direction. Just outside of his Mrs. Friedman's history classroom, Isaiah came across Karen.

"Hey Karen," said Isaiah. "How've you been?"

"Ummm...hi," said Karen. She was lukewarm at best. "Were you just talking to Tyler Base again?"

"Yeah," said Isaiah. "I was telling him I don't think I'll write for him anymore."

"Good," Karen said with a curt nod. "So what's up?"

"Not much," said Isaiah. "Just wanted to see how you were doing. Things have been pretty crazy lately."

"I'm fine Isaiah," she said. "You don't need to check up on me." Karen seemed to recall something. "I'll admit one thing. The *Gates Times* is going too far. Remember that boy Timothy?"

"Yeah," said Isaiah. "He wrote the neutral review of Hamlet for the *Gates Sentinel*." While the positive and negative review had both drawn backlash, Timothy had avoided attention so far. "What about him?"

"Some kids in the lunch line were talking smack about him," said Karen. "How he supposedly had the flu during one of the football games and somebody also claimed that they saw him laughing with a group of other students when Tyler told a joke about the Splat."

"Who were the gossipers?" asked Isaiah.

"A bunch of upperclassman girls," said Karen. "Dawn Appleton was one of them." Dawn was a veteran gossip columnist. "She said she supposedly heard that Timothy was peeping in the girl's locker room and that she was going to write about that rumor in her next article."

"Dawn's in my English class," said Isaiah. "I never liked her much, even before this year."

"I told them to leave Timothy alone," Karen went on. "I don't want anyone to be toxic, but Timothy tutored me last year when I fell behind in Pre-Calc. He's a really sweet kid."

"Gossip columns should never have started," said Isaiah. "It's not like school gossip was never a problem before, but having one or two gossip narratives shoved down our throats really is...toxic."

"Why don't school reporters just report the truth?" Karen wondered aloud.

"The *Gates Times* used to do that on their own," said Isaiah. "If school reporting would just give us the facts, everyone could interpret it their own way. But if opinions, commentary and gossip seep into the reporting then gossip becomes magnified and spins out of control."

"Right," Karen said with a nod. She was friendlier now. "Everyone could gossip almost as though everyone were their own school newspaper, but their influence would be much more limited."

"Exactly," said Isaiah. "The In Crowd claims that a school newspaper has to do this in order to fight gossip and toxicity. Instead, all we see is high schoolers acting like they're in elementary school again. Seriously Karen, did you ever imagine teenagers acting the way kids at Gates are right now?"

"Never in a million years," said Karen. "Imagine if grown adults were behaving that way."

Isaiah laughed for the first time since the confrontation in the principal's office. "That may be going a bit far." As chaotic as this school year had proven to be, Karen's joke painted a picture far more absurd.

"I wish everyone would talk to each other like we are now," said Karen.

Isaiah agreed. "Nobody's acting their age right now. It really is like we've regressed all the way back to elementary school."

"Not surprising with Shelly and Tyler constantly in the background."

"I'm glad that we agree on this, Karen," said Isaiah. "Everett wouldn't."

"Huh?" said Karen. "Why do you say that Isaiah? Everett's reasonable. You should give him more credit."

"I would like to," said Isaiah. "I really would, but he's been giving me bad vibes. Whenever I try to engage him he seems to back away." Isaiah didn't want to dwell on it. "Tyler says he's still going to continue the *Gates Sentinel*, even after all that's happened."

"I see," said Karen. "You used to write for them, didn't you? Don't tell me you wrote some of those awful gossip columns."

"No, no," Isaiah assured her. "I never wrote gossip columns for them. Mostly I wrote on how to stay in shape and talked a little about my weightlifting routine from over the summer."

"I see," said Karen.

"Figured I'd write down some tips that would've been good for me to know as a freshman," he went on. "Somebody else might find them useful. I did know some of the gossip columnists for the *Gates Sentinel*, though. The majority of them said that they first started in reaction to one of the gossip columns in the *Gates Times*."

"Even if the *Gates Times* publishes disgusting gossip stories, that's no excuse for sinking to their level," said Karen. "Gossip columns, rival gossip columns, no end in sight. This makes me want to speed up time and graduate as soon as possible."

"I know," Isaiah said with a nod. "I wish that Hallie never started this."

"What's that supposed to mean?" asked Karen. "Even if her reaction is over the top, that doesn't excuse what people say about her."

"Believe me, I have nothing personal against Hallie," said Isaiah. "She was in a pretty embarrassing situation when that break-up letter got posted in a blog for all to see. I get that. I really do. Since then, however, she's handled it in completely the wrong way. Targeting uninvolved third parties and asking the *Gates Times* to run gossip columns for her has only added fuel to the flames."

The bell rang. "Listen Isaiah, I need to get to class. We can talk later."

"Break-ups aren't fun," Isaiah went on. "You and I both know that, and Hallie's clearly not having fun in her own. A lot of troubled words go back and forth. She can still do the right thing by letting this fall behind her and move on in life. Her toxic environment is becoming a self-fulfilling prophecy. Besides, if you want to talk about what's justified and what isn't just look at what she's doing to the whole Out Crowd. None of that is justified, regardless of what she's been through."

Karen had already left and went to class. Normally, Isaiah would be annoyed that she left him alone while he was in the middle of having a conversation with her. He was not alone, however. There was someone standing where Karen had been a minute before, but it wasn't her.

It was Antenor.

Isaiah's immediate worries formed in his brain as Antenor towered over him. He did not know exactly how long he had been standing there, but Antenor looked like he had been standing there long enough.

Antenor seized Isaiah by the collar of his shirt and swung him into the locker behind him four times before shoving him to the ground and kicking him repeatedly. Drops of blood fell from Isaiah's face to the floor as he lay there scrambling to get away and back to his feet.

They were only interrupted by one of the school security guards who came by on one of his regular patrols of the hallway. "Leave us," the security guard said to Antenor. "There's no fighting allowed in school." Antenor marched off, fuming and breathing heavily with every step he took. The security guard then turned to Isaiah. "What was that all about? Did you say something toxic?"

"No," said Isaiah. "He just attacked me out of nowhere."

The security guard was skeptical. "I don't think he would have done that unless you said something toxic to catch his attention. Wait a second – what's that?" The security guard noticed the edge of the *Gates Sentinel* with its Teddy the Toad logo sticking out from Isaiah's binder. "You're carrying banned toxic material here." At this point many other students stood around Isaiah and the security guard, pointing at the former and whispering. "I'm sending you home," the security guard told Isaiah. "You're suspended for the rest of the day and you're to report to Mr. Zee's computer classroom for detention after school." He took a look at Isaiah's bleeding. "This is your first offense. I guess that I'll let you pay a visit to the school nurse on your way out the door." With that, the security guard left Isaiah behind, who was still trying to get to his feet.

"Can someone help me up?" he said.

A nearby junior girl shot him a look. "I think you can handle that by yourself."

It took almost a full minute for Isaiah to hoist his aching body into a standing position. No sooner than he had was he punched in the face again. "Jeff?" he said, noticing his new assailant's face. "You too, Jeff?"

"Sorry about this," Jeff whispered as he punched him again. Last spring Jeff and Isaiah had been lab partners in biology class. They had never been close friends, but they always got along just fine. "It's nothing personal," Jeff said as he punched Isaiah in the face a third time. "Ever since this sitting with the In Crowd thing started I've wanted to take a turn with them myself, but I've never had a chance. This is my chance, Isaiah."

"Drop dead," Isaiah spat, still too weak to fight back.

"Alright, I can't be seen talking to you anymore," said Jeff, slugging Isaiah one more time in the face. "Mr. Smith," Jeff said as the shop teacher passed them by. "How are you doing?"

"Stop this," said Mr. Smith. "There's no fighting in school. Why were you punching him?"

"Because he's toxic," explained Jeff. "I always punch people I think are toxic. I just can't help myself."

"Well…" Mr. Smith said, uneasy with the situation. "Jeff, be that as it may, you can't just go around punching people. I'm going to need you to practice some self control."

"I'll try," Jeff said, "but I can't make any promises."

Chapter 14: Detention

Isaiah left in a hurry the next morning, so was not able to eat breakfast. He had fully recovered from his injuries, apart from the bruises. Initially, he thought he could eat a lot at lunch to make up for skipping breakfast earlier. However, Mr. Zee, the computer teacher, chose to meet with Isaiah during lunch hour. Mr. Zee had summoned Isaiah to his office to discuss his afternoon detention.

Although he knew he had done nothing wrong, Isaiah apologized for his actions. Mr. Zee told Isaiah he had done the right thing, and that he would have only one afternoon of detention instead of two. Isaiah was shocked that he had almost gotten two days of detention, but relieved that he had dodged that bullet. Nevertheless, he promised himself that he would be more careful in the future. From this point on, Isaiah would not speak up if he saw anything he felt off about, but would keep his head down. The last thing he needed to do was suffer more just because of his pride.

Everything around Gates High was now constantly changing. Principal Terrence was enacting new school policies almost on a daily basis. The confrontation in his office ended the way it did as part of his attempt to satisfy the In Crowd, but since that pivotal day the In Crowd had only increased their pressure to meld the school in their image. Policies changed from day to day so hardly anybody in the Out Crowd could keep track of them anymore, even Hallie Flynn's staunchest defenders. Regardless, not being aware of a new policy was no excuse for not being able to follow it to the letter.

One of the junior football players also wrote for the *Gates Times*. His most recent opinion piece drew a lot of attention.

> I understand that this is not how everyone likes to see things done, but even if Antenor, T-Bone and Farouk use ugly means, they do achieve the end of stopping people from behaving toxically. I don't see how any reasonable person could object to that. If you find yourself uncomfortable with what Antenor, T-Bone and Farouk are doing, you should probably examine your intentions. Do you really object that much to the way they confront toxicity, or is it merely the fact that they're confronting toxicity to begin with? If you object to their confronting people who spread toxic rumors more than you object to the people saying those toxic things, you must have some internalized toxicity yourself. That's your cue to acknowledge that you are part of the. Go visit one of the guidance counselors if you're too confused to handle it on your own. We have four of them for a reason.

Isaiah reported to Mr. Zee's detention classroom after school. Mr. Zee was the computer teacher, but he had unplugged all of the computers as soon as the bell rang. It would be nice to turn them on, browse the web or play a game, but that was not an option in detention.

Isaiah's stomach growled at him the entirety of his detention. Skipping both breakfast and lunch was catching up to him.

He had only been given detention once before, during sophomore year for cutting Algebra 101, but he noticed right away how different it was now. The classroom was full. There had never been enough kids given detention to fill the classroom up before. A few of them were in there for "traditional" reasons such as cheating on a test, cutting class or smoking outside. The rest of them were all in there for exercising "toxic" behaviors.

Last year, Antenor, T-Bone and Farouk had all been amongst the most frequent customers of Mr. Zee for all the fighting and beating up other kids in school. This year, all three of them did that more than ever, but they never got detention for it. In fact, the Gates High faculty and all the school security guards seemed to be actively avoiding giving them detention as long as everything they did was in the name of making their school environment less toxic.

Isaiah sat quietly in his desk for the entire detention period, recognizing a few faces among the others in the classroom. Tyler Base had done something to get detention. Isaiah had not seen what it was, nor was he surprised to find Tyler in his company.

Dan from Dungeons and Dragons Club was sitting in one of the seats. This came as a surprise after Dan had taken a very "anti-toxic" tune earlier in the year. He was the one who snitched on the "toxic" spray-painters and got invited to a party at Hallie's house as a reward. Now he had clearly done something the In Crowd didn't like, which was a full one-eighty for him. Since Dan didn't talk much, it was largely unknown what had changed his mind.

Yazidi, the new girl, was there as well. She had given her newspaper article to the *Gates Sentinel* after the *Gates Times* decided not to publish it. However, the *Gates Times* claimed that by submitting it to them Yazidi had given them exclusive rights to the story. Subsequently submitting it to another publication violated those exclusive rights.

There was nothing to do but wait it out. By the time detention was over Isaiah was starving. He was ready to devour the first edible piece of matter he came across, even if it was moldy bread. By the time he got home Isaiah would have even settled for moldy breadcrumbs.

Isaiah also had difficulty his appetite the following day. As usual, the *Gates Times* was being distributed in the cafeteria.

The Gates Times; Volume 69, Issue 29

From the Editor: Happy Fall Harvest!

Mr. Smith the shop teacher recently pointed out that a number of claims in our previous gossip columns were unverified. Deputy Editor Zach O'Phant and I attempted to reason with him, but Mr. Smith actually went as far as to say he would speak to Mrs. Friedman and the principal if we did not differentiate between fact and opinion. Ms. Eden the English teacher and former faculty advisor to a certain other student organization swooped in and backed him up. We at the *Gates Times* were forced to reach a compromise and from this point onward we will use the phrase "if true" when writing our gossip columns. For instance, instead of saying: "Sharon is spreading toxic gossip; Sharon is toxic," we will be forced to say, "Sharon is spreading toxic gossip; If true, Sharon is toxic," which resolves any perceived issue of uncertainty.

Shelly Boudin, Editor-in-Chief

Isaiah happened to be standing behind Shelly in the lunch line.

"Was this really necessary?" Shelly whispered to her Deputy Editor. "Mr. Smith didn't seem entirely satisfied when our staff told him of our solution."

"I know," Zach O'Phant, a junior boy, nodded in agreement. "He doesn't seem to like us very much. In this chaotic time it is so demoralizing that a teacher doesn't understand our need to combat toxicity. If a grown man doesn't get it, what message does that send when we try to inform our fellow students?"

"I know," said Shelly. "I mean, it's not the worst thing in the world to add a couple words every now and then. Why do we need that extra burden, though? We've got enough on our plate as it is."

"It's awful," said Zach.

"They're making our jobs more difficult," said Shelly. "Some kids keep telling me we need to change our approach and try to connect with students better, but I don't see how we're supposed to do that. I guess we need to just keep on writing more gossip columns and eventually the school will be less toxic."

"I couldn't agree more," said Zach. "The *Gates Sentinel* always did too much thinking outside the box. You saw where that led them. We cannot return to the dark days when unwanted gossip stood on an equal footing with more desirable gossip. The *Gates Times'* mission is to set the unsophisticated Out Crowders straight, and that's what we need to do."

"Thanks, Zach," said Shelly. "You never do have any good ideas of your own, but you always know when to confirm my ideas whenever I'm on the verge of second-guessing myself."

"That's exceptionally easy, Shelly," said Zach. "Your ideas are always good."

"You flatter me," said Shelly. "It's your unwavering loyalty which gives me the courage to stay the course at times like these."

"I am only happy to help you serve the GHS community."

Isaiah stared at the day's menu for longer than normal. It took all the willpower he had to resist the urge to butt his way into the conversation in front of him.

Chapter 15: Falling Out

At lunch the following day, Isaiah's former lab partner Jeff had finally taken his seat among the In Crowd. More visiting Out Crowders were there today than ever before. They had all stroked the egos of the In Crowders in some way in order to get their seat. Likewise, the In Crowders stroked the egos of their visitors and allowed them to enjoy their time amongst them. The visitors also signaled their temporary glory to their fellow Out Crowders. The signalers and the In Crowd were a perfect match for each other in this egotistical strokefest. Forces much larger than the In Crowd - or even Gates High itself - had brought them together.

Since the *Gates Times* now held an official monopoly on school gossip, rumors became monotonous and this in turn pumped more one-sided fuel into the signaling and the stroking. Jeff in particular relished his stroking moment, and did his best to magnify his signal. Isaiah's former lab partner turned toward the rest of the cafeteria and made eye contact with as many Out Crowders as he could. He skipped over Isaiah.

Since today's congregation was so large, Jeff only managed to squeeze into one of the farther corners. He was nowhere near Joel or Hallie, but he struck up a conversation with the junior cheerleader sitting next to him. Actually, it wasn't much of a conversation. He talked. She ignored. Eventually she got up and left.

"Why so glum, Isaiah?" Everett asked his friend. "Here, check this out. The *Gates Times* added back their funnies section. I know that you used to like them."

"Wait, I thought that Shelly Boudin said she wasn't doing the funnies anymore because she things were too serious now."

"She did say that Isaiah," said Everett. "And I agreed with her at the time, but apparently she decided to bring them back after all."

Isaiah took the newspaper from Everett's hands. "This isn't what I would call funny, Everett. It's only one comic and it's just a picture of three monkeys." The one on the left had his hands covering his eyes, the one in the center was covering his ears and the one on the right was covering his mouth.

Everett pointed beneath the comic. "You haven't read the caption yet."

Isaiah sighed. "Monkey see no toxicity," he read aloud. "Monkey hear no toxicity. Monkey speak no toxicity. Yeah, I'm still not getting the punch line, Everett."

"Man, those toxic people must have really messed you up," Everett told Isaiah. "You don't even understand comedy anymore. You know, if you'd just kept your mouth shut, Antenor wouldn't have tracked you down and you wouldn't have gotten detention."

"Are you saying what I did was toxic and deserving of that?" asked Isaiah. "If that was toxic, then go ahead and call me toxic. You know, Everett, if Antenor had come after you for saying something I would have defended you."

Everett scoffed. "Don't be ridiculous. It's that same foolish attitude that got you beaten up in the first place. Maybe you ought to examine yourself a little more."

"Are you trying to sit with the In Crowd, Everett?" asked Craig.

Everett shrugged. "It'd be nice, but they've never noticed my meager contributions against the toxic environment. Maybe it's for the best. I want to be sure I'm being anti-toxic for the right reasons and not just for the perks."

Karen came over. "Craig, I need to ask you something."

"Sure."

"Don't talk to Karen," Everett said to Craig. "Didn't you read the *Gates Times* gossip columns this morning? She's toxic."

"Excuse me?" Karen said to Everett. "It's all lies. I never-"

Everett held up a hand to shut her up. "If you continue talking to her, Craig, people may start calling you toxic, too."

Isaiah was astonished. "What's your problem Everett?"

"What's my problem?" said Everett. "I'm doing what is best for all of us. Karen might've been a friend or girlfriend to some of us, but that's in the past now. We need to make sure we don't become toxic too." Everett narrowed his eyes. "And you're getting pretty close, Isaiah."

"No," said Isaiah, standing up. "I won't let anyone else tell me who to talk to or not talk to."

"I'm with Isaiah on this," said Craig. However, he remained seating and did not raise his voice. "Karen's a friend. I'll talk to her whatever people say about her."

"Thanks Craig," said Karen. "I appreciate that."

Everett pointed away from the table. "Go Karen," said Everett. "You heard me before. You're not a very nice person."

"No Karen, don't go anywhere," Isaiah said loud enough for people at the next table over to stare. "Everett, get up." He clenched his fists.

"No Isaiah," said Karen. "It's fine. You don't have to do anything." She left before any of the trio at the table could say anything.

Neither Isaiah, nor Everett or Craig said another word that lunch.

* * *

When lunch was over, the entire student body was called to the auditorium. Principal Terrence was subjecting them to the first ever "sensitivity assembly" at Gates High. Everyone was required to attend, and from that day onward they would be held as often as it was deemed necessary.

"For those of you bringing toxicity and cruelty wherever you go," Principal Terrence said to students in the sensitivity assembly, "I tell you this. You are not welcome here. Gates High School is a welcoming environment for non-toxic individuals to come together free of toxic people such as yourself. The leaders among our student body are rising to the challenge. Hallie Flynn and Joel Boudin have been vigorous about uncovering toxicity wherever it arises and bringing it to my attention so that appropriate consequences can be levied. Then we also have Shelly Boudin, Joel's twin sister who runs the *Gates Times* and has been spreading awareness about toxicity and dealing with the toxic elements that are permeating our school environment.

"You know, I was at a conference this past weekend with other school administrators. I explained to them everything that was going on here at Gates High this year and they told me none of them had ever dealt with anything like it. I'm in the same boat.

This is all new to me, too. I'm used to dealing with every problem that comes up at school myself. That is my job, after all, as principal. As far as this toxicity stuff goes, though, it seems only right for me to step back and let you kids lead the way forward."

* * *

"Isaiah, you haven't been honest with me," Everett said the next time they ate lunch together.

"Huh?" said Isaiah. "What makes you say that?"

Everett read aloud from the school newspaper. "Isaiah yelled toxic lines in the middle of the hallway, frightening many of the students around him with his uncontrollable rage. Jeff, his former lab partner, pleaded with his old friend, begging him to stop, but Isaiah would not listen. He proceeded to whip out a tall stack of contraband *Gates Sentinel* newspapers and shove them in the faces of unsuspecting underclassmen. It was only when Antenor exposed this and reported him to the Gates High faculty that Isaiah's toxic tirade was finally stopped. He was immediately given detention for the rest of the week, making GHS a safer environment for all. It remains to be seen whether Isaiah has truly learned his lesson or if he will repeat his toxic actions later on, but for now, the student body can breathe a little bit easier."

Isaiah spat the peas out of his mouth. "That's not how it happened," he protested.

"Don't lie to me, Isaiah. I'm holding the *Gates Times* right here in my hand. Maybe if you watched your words more you wouldn't have gotten roughed up. Everett recalled something else. "Isaiah, you danced with that girl Claire at Homecoming," said Everett. "An entire room full of Gates girls and you decided to dance with the one from Byzantine High School. Isaiah, is there anything else you're not telling us?"

"Are you serious?" Isaiah asked, his disbelief now greater than it had been all year. "Everett, you were there. You saw how I wound up dancing with Claire. It had nothing to do with a conspiracy with Byzantine High School."

"I also remember something else," Everett said, ignoring his friend's objections. "You as good as admitted to spying for Byzantine High last Black Friday."

"I was being sarcastic!"

"Sarcasm, huh? How convenient. Don't gaslight me, Isaiah. You are cornered."

"Everett, Isaiah's got a point," Craig interjected before Isaiah could respond. "What he said was perfectly reasonable; certainly nothing to send enforcers attacking him over. The *Gates Times* is becoming just as bad as the *Gates Sentinel* was, maybe even worse."

"How could you say that?" Everett asked him. "I expected better from you, Craig."

"Look, I acknowledge that being toxic is a problem," said Craig. "Maybe even a widespread problem, but the school is taking it the wrong way. People on both sides are being ridiculous. Maybe there are a lot of toxic people out there causing problems, but members of the In Crowd are toxic as well."

"No they aren't," said Everett. "That's ridiculous."

Craig wasn't backing down today. "Are you actually telling me that what Isaiah did was toxic, but sending Antenor after him wasn't toxic, and throwing him into detention with all the other kids in there wasn't toxic either?"

"Of course," said Everett. "The methods are only strong because they have to be, and toxicity doesn't have to be out of the open. Even casual toxicity and complacency with toxic behavior is still just as bad as the worst kind of being toxic."

Craig raised an eyebrow. "So you're telling me that thinking 'toxic' thoughts is just as bad everything the *Gates Times* says in their gossip columns, even when its made up?"

"Yes," Everett declared without any hesitation.

"Let me get this straight," Craig continued. "Certain non-toxic people call things toxic, and we shouldn't question them. Questioning them is toxic. I see clear double standards with which gossip columns are toxic and which are not. Criticizing the *Gates Times* or the In Crowd is apparently off limits. Saying someone is to blame for problems they're dealing with is toxic. Saying someone is innocent after they've been accused of being toxic is also toxic. Laughing at people who were falsely called toxic is not toxic, but is part of the solution. 'Verbal violence' is always toxic, but actual violence isn't always toxic even if it is misguided."

"You've got it," said Everett. "What's the problem?"

"I see," said Craig. "Well, what exactly is it that makes the difference, Everett? Can you explain this 'toxicity' to me?"

Everett upended his lunch tray, spilling it all on the table. "I don't believe this!" he exclaimed, rising to his feet. "I'm out of here. I can no longer be associated with either one of you." Storming off, he left both Isaiah and Craig behind.

"Who is he going to sit with?" Craig asked Isaiah. "We're his two best friends."

"We *were* his two best friends," Isaiah corrected him. "I don't know. Beats me."

* * *

Across the cafeteria Hallie and Joel were throwing ideas back and forth with each other. Shelly sat with them for this. "What about that kid Isaiah?" Hallie said to the Boudins. "Did you hear what he said about me to get detention the other day? I think he should go in one of our gossip columns again next issue."

"Sure," Joel said with a shrug. "Why not."

Shelly was scrambling to keep everything organized. "These toxic people really cannot get over how cool and pretty you are, Hallie."

"How many are left?" Hallie asked her.

"A lot," said Shelly. "We're still on Eddy. What should we say about him?"

"I don't know," said Hallie. "Say that they were seen texting on their phone with Byzantine High Schoolers about our football strategy."

"We use the BHS angle a lot," Shelly said.

Hallie shrugged. "So?"

"If it ain't broke, don't fix it," said Joel.

"I don't want to be too repetitive," Shelly said as she formed her own thoughts. "I think we could use some more…variation. Yes, variation would be good."

Hallie rolled her eyes. "Fine. Say something else about Eddy."

"Like what?" said Joel.

"Say he hits on middle schoolers," Hallie suggested.

"Yea," Joel concurred. "Just go with that. Whatever."

Shelly sighed. "Okay, that'll work for now, but we'll need fresh material for the next gossip cycle. We can only rehash old rumors so much."

Hallie shrugged. "It seems to be working out so far. Do you guys want to come over after school to brainstorm some more?"

"Can't," said Joel. "I'm heading the ninth grader's lounge after the last bell rings. I'm taking Veronica out for our fourth anniversary tonight."

"Ah, alright," said Hallie. "Have fun."

"You could come to our house sometime this week," Shelly suggested. "Or we could always brainstorm at lunch again."

"Sure," said Hallie. "Whatever works."

* * *

The following Saturday Gates had a football game against Northern Central High School. Attending football games had been compulsory for some time now, but that did not mean that any past toxic boycotters were forgiven. Joel Boudin's touchdown dances had grown longer than ever and they now routinely went on for several minutes.

Warm weather was disappearing. The football players wore long sleeves underneath their uniforms and the cheerleaders wore GHS jackets over theirs. Except, of course, when they were performing.

As the team leaders persisted, though, so did the toxicity. They were greeted with a chorus of toxic boos from the toxic booers at the audience. Hallie and Joel ignored them, even as the length of the game doubled and they were forced to deal with a toxic audience twice as long.

The Gates Times; Volume 69, Issue 35

Gates High School versus Northern Central High School

Independent estimates show that Joel's dances now take up so much time that they lengthen the time students are required to sit and watch the game by as much as thirty percent. Isn't it great Joel's giving us such an extra treat? Hallie Flynn shows off her best cheerleading moves in the meantime. Just before half time, Joel and Hallie did a duet series of cartwheels across the field together.

Choruses of toxic groans were heard in the audience during the longest touchdown dance. The *Gates Times* provides you with verified gossip you can trust to counter such noise. Today, that reliable gossip states that GHS as a whole enjoy Joel's dances very much, and that allegedly loud chorus was only a few disgruntled fans voicing their toxicity. Let us all do the right thing and not give such toxic sentiments the validation they desire. Punching the air has been a noticeable addition to the Gates captain's regular dance routines. So what does it mean when Joel Boudin throws these jabs and uppercuts at the air? Why, he's pretending to punch toxic people.

"Punching toxic people" is a phrase most of the GHS community has heard by now. Some students we interviewed have misgivings about it. That's somewhat understandable.

After all, if actual violence isn't toxic, then what is? We won't be quoting any of those students directly, since that would spread their misguided logic. What we will do is use this as a teaching moment for them and for anyone else with similar reservations. Yes, it is wrong to advocate violence against anyone, no matter who they are. It is always correct to oppose violence, but if you oppose violence against toxic people, that means you are in fact supporting those toxic people. Therefore, to oppose punching toxic people is to be toxic yourself. You're not toxic, are you? Good. Then you support punching toxic people. End of discussion.

As soon as the game was over, everybody went straight home. Northern Central High School was closer to Gates than any other school in Western County. In prior seasons both football teams and their cheerleading squads had always gone out as a big group for pizza after they played each other, but no one from any other high school wanted anything to do with Gates High Schoolers anymore.

Chapter 16: The Hacking

The week after the game against Northern Central, the website for the *Gates Times* got hacked. All of the real articles and gossip columns were replaced by pieces that resembled the rival gossip columns of the *Gates Sentinel*. The site's coding was altered and the headlines were in various fonts and flashy colors. Honking noise emitted whenever one clicked on one of the hyperlinks.

The New Gates Times; Volume 777, Issue XXX

From the New Editor

How do you like our new look? We decided that it was time to give this news site more flair to shake things up a bit. Sadly though, there is some dreadful news today. Shelly Boudin has stepped down after a long career in the rigorous world of high school news.

Shelly's distinguishing achievements include introducing gossip columns and drawing attention to the ongoing toxic epidemic. She did not stop at covering such epidemic with just one story, but filled entire issues multiple days in a row with discussion of toxic rumors. As a matter of fact, she created a lot of the story to begin with. Now that takes reporting to a whole nother level. Let's look no further than Shelly Boudin for an example of how to make the news what you want it to be.

Teddy the Toad will be taking her place. Filling Shelly's shoes won't be an easy task. Prior to Shelly's editorship, the *Gates Times* was held back by old-fashioned journalistic traditions like verifying information and even avoiding school gossip altogether. However, Teddy remains confident he'll make some progress of his own. After all, he has the historic distinction as the first mascot to run a school newspaper.

Until today, every news editor in Gates High history has been a student, so it's about time mascots got the representation they deserve.

Since when does a school have to be for students only?

Teddy, Lord Chancellor of the Gates Sentinel and President of Teddy's Universe

Teddy the Toad's image replaced the GHS logo in the top banner and "Teddy" was listed as the author of every article. This was presumably so those who actually wrote the articles remained anonymous.

Under the tab where the *Gates Times* funnies would usually be, there was a cartoon featuring Teddy. The Crying Kitties did not accompany him today. Instead, there were unmistakable drawings of Antenor, T-Bone and Farouk chasing after Teddy.

The penultimate panel showed Teddy hiding behind a door while the trio searched for him. In the last panel, Teddy emerged and tackled all three of them at once.

Probably the boldest article was a gossip column about the In Crowd's three chief enforcers. "Just how many grades have Antenor, T-Bone and Farouk been held back?" the article asked rhetorically. "Even though they're all still in high school, it turns out, these guys are well into their twenties." The article went on to say that they also continued to wet their pants on occasion. During the summer, they were alleged to have stolen money from the poor box at a local church to spend on partying.

One of the other rival gossip columns was unique, to say the least. Like the others, the author was anonymous, but it read like a member of the Dungeons and Dragons Club wrote it.

> Hallie Flynn is not really a cheerleader. She merely takes the form of one. In fact, she is an evil witch, but that's a secret she doesn't want anyone to know about. This past week, she tried to torture some kids in her dungeon when they found out the truth. One of them escaped though, and now everyone will learn her horrible secret.
>
> At the beginning of this year the witch Hallie Flynn placed the entire Land of Gates High under one of her wicked enchantments. This spell was reinforced by the tyrannical rule of her orc army, led by General Joel Boudin.
>
> Slowly, however, the inhabitants of Gates High are awakening from her enchantment one at a time. Hallie is desperate because

even she lacks the power to stop this. Once
somebody is no longer under her spell,
there's no going back. As time runs out, she
is determined to resist this great awakening
until the very end.

Shelly Boudin found out about the hacking soon after it
happened, but it took a few hours to revert the site to normal.
Not only did the hackers change the password of the site, but they
had hacked Shelly's personal email and changed the password
there as well. No one knew who had hacked the site and there
was little to no evidence floating around, but that didn't prevent
Mr. Zee from giving Tyler Base an unprecedented thirty days in
detention for allegedly being the supposed mastermind.

In the actual *Gates Times* issue released the following day,
Shelly Boudin addressed the hacking.

The Gates Times; Volume 69, Issue 36

From the Editor: Setting the Record Straight

For those who are still confused, no I
have not resigned. I am still very much
the head of Gates High's only active news
publication. Last night a certain person
- quite possibly from a certain former
school newspaper - hacked our website
and inserted a load of false stories in place
of our actual articles. This is merely the
latest shenanigan in a smear campaign that
me and the newspaper I run are dedicated
to fighting.

There ought to be a rule against circumventing school newspapers and posting unauthorized gossip on the Internet. Clearly such an action would not be possible unless there was outside help involved. Byzantine High School spies are by far the most likely perpetrators. Anyone at Gates who continues to deny this reality is unwittingly allowing themselves to become toxic and opening themselves up to being called out as such.

Thanks to this reckless prank I was forced to summon the entire staff of our *legitimate* newspaper to my house. Everyone had to crank out a minimum of two new articles each just to respond to the pseudo-issue. I myself only had time to scribble this genuine message from the editor. Just before ten o'clock I baked cookies to show appreciation for my staff, then went straight to bed. Everyone else, however, was awake until at least two. Many of them had homework to do on top of it.

I would've stayed up with them, but I have a hunch Mr. Dyson would give my class a pop quiz in the morning and if that's the case then I need a good night's sleep for that. He probably won't, but better safe than sorry. You all know who the *Gates Times* reporters are. Look at them as you pass them in the hall today. See how exhausted they are? Well that's the damage that this hacker has caused.

Shelly Boudin, Editor-in-Chief

Half a dozen gossip columns were dedicated to describing different ways that Byzantine High Schoolers may have perpetrated the hacking. Another gossip column addressed the hackers' cartoon.

> I can't believe I have to report on this. Yesterday hackers who broke into the Gates Times website posted a comic featuring toxic symbol Teddy the Toad alongside depictions of three of our classmates. Teddy was shown to be running from such students and subsequently tackling them. Readers of the now-defunct *Gates Sentinel* are reportedly claiming that it was a funny cartoon and go on to point out that Teddy was acting in self-defense. Yes. You read that correctly. Members of the student body here at Gates are legitimizing violence against Antenor, T-Bone and Farouk. Even worse, they mischaracterize Antenor, T-Bone and Farouk's completely legitimate resistance to the toxic environment suppressing Gates High.
>
> Dawn Appleton, Gates Times Correspondent

Hallie was also quoted about the cartoon. "These hackers weren't simply performing a harmless prank," she said. "They were inciting violence against three football players constantly doing everything they can to make the school a better place. Antenor, T-Bone and Farouk were the main victims of the hacking scandal." Hallie Flynn's interviews in the *Gates Times* became more and more frequent.

The rogue story from the hacking that got the most attention was the lengthy gossip column on Antenor, T-Bone and Farouk. An entire section from the *Gates Times* was dedicated to who the anonymous author was. Five possible suspects were speculated about in different gossip columns. The hype surrounding who the author was, though, did not last long, since Antenor, T-Bone and Farouk simply beat up all five of the possible suspects that day.

"I wish I had time to read all the articles from the hacked website before they took them down," Isaiah lamented later on.

Karen held up her cell phone. "I got them all screenshotted on here. Let me text them to you."

Some students from the Mock Trial Team and the Checkers Club came together and attempted to start a third school newspaper, the *Gates Weekly Journal*. Their plan had been to focus on stories that the *Gates Times* used to focus on, so that students could follow events surrounding school activities, changes in school policies and upcoming school-sponsored initiatives going on. In their founding charter, the staff of the *Gates Weekly Journal* pledged to focus exclusively on objective news stories (no gossip columns), to take no sides and to treat every member of the GHS community with dignity and respect. Regardless, it was shut down before ever publishing a single issue.

* * *

They *Gates Weekly Journal* were not the only ones starting a brand new student organization over the fall, and others had better luck. A savory clique of underclassmen started the first-ever Anti-Toxicity League chapter at Gates High. Even though it was founded and run by underclassmen, they did not hesitate to name Hallie Flynn their honorary Founder, President and Chairwoman.

Anti-Toxicity League activities consisted of lurking around school, investigating who was exhibiting signs of toxic behavior and cataloguing all the information at their meetings, creating handouts to give to curious fellow students. A long-term goal of theirs was giving handouts to incoming freshmen when the time came so that they too would become aware of the problems that toxic people were causing.

Once the information was compiled, the members of the Anti-Toxicity League would report their findings to Editor-in-Chief Shelly Boudin, so that she could in turn pass along the results of their research to her staff writers for inclusion in upcoming gossip columns. Thus, a lasting partnership between the Anti-Toxicity League and the *Gates Times* was born.

Or at least that was what the Anti-Toxicity League did for everyone except the very worst of offenders. For those who were the most toxic and carried the most signs with them, they went straight to Shelly's twin brother instead. On these occasions, Joel Boudin always assured them that he would make sure that Antenor, T-Bone and Farouk were aware.

Chapter 17: Untouchables

The layout of the *Gates Times* had changed a lot. As a part of the school's efforts to combat toxicity, the school newspaper was handed out to every student in homeroom now. The front-page section always contained the most relevant and interesting stories of the day. Since Shelly made her most recent round of changes, the front section was perpetually filled with gossip columns about seniors.

The sports section was traditionally the next one in. Until this year all the sports in season would have their schedules posted along with the outcomes and commentary on the games themselves. Football was still talked about some. Other fall sports such as soccer, rugby, cross-country and field hockey got no coverage, as gossip columns about juniors filled the section.

Then there was the section that used to be the opinion section. Here, any student could express their opinions on current events going on in the world, events going on in school or comment on a piece of pop culture. The section still featured opinions of a sort, but they were all expressed in the form of gossip columns about sophomores.

Arts and Entertainment had always been run in the next section, where one would find stories about related matters. Today, however, it was only gossip columns about freshmen.

The final section was where the ever-popular funnies were always found in the past, along with games like Sudoku, Word Searches and Crossword puzzles. This fall, it had become the section for gossip columns about Untouchables. The Untouchables were a new classification given to specific students at Gates High who demonstrated the highest levels of toxicity. Unlike those who were written about in gossip columns for the first time, there was no question of how toxic they were. Shelly Boudin allowed only her most experienced and elite writers contribute to this section. Less experienced writers and guest columnists always had to contribute to one of the other four sections. Unless, of course, the guest columnist was Hallie Flynn. Yes, Hallie herself occasionally wrote articles now.

In fact, it was Hallie who had coined the term Untouchables for the first time in her own gossip column, when she needed a stronger word than "toxic" or "deplorable." Shelly encouraged other writers to use it as well, and the term soon caught on. After Hallie met with Principal Terrence one day, Gates High created new school policies, and the principal's office kept their own up-to-date list of those who held the Untouchable designation.

Untouchables were ostracized from student life in a number of ways. They were typically seen frequently in detention with Mr. Zee and were prime targets for Antenor, T-Bone and Farouk. Gates High School had recently hired more security guards, doubling the size of their force, and they always kept a close eye on those who were labeled "Untouchable." Some of the new security guards were only part-time or had other jobs. Principal Terrence would take whatever he could get in his desperate response to the Toxicity Crisis.

Untouchables were also banned from the school nurse, banned from ever sitting at the In Crowd's tables and banned from the school guidance counselors. It was a convenient time to decrease the volume of students going to high school therapy. Guidance Counselor Jones had been caught drinking on the job in between sessions, so he had just been let go. Gates dropped back down to three school guidance counselors, and Principal Terrence used the additional money saved to hire new security guards instead.

Shelly interviewed Principal Terrence for the *Gates Times* personally. He did not disclose what further action was being considered, but he made a point that "anything and everything" would be kicked up a notch.

Isaiah received a notice in homeroom. With no reason given, he had been given detention again. During lunch hour he reported to Mr. Zee's office. He stood in line behind Tyler Base.

"Hey Isaiah," Tyler greeted. "Well, looks like we're both back in high school jail once again."

"I don't want to make a habit of this, Tyler," said Isaiah. "I just want to get this over with and move on with my life."

"So you're going to apologize then?"

"Yes," confirmed Isaiah. "I'd rather just have one day of detention. I don't even know what I'm here for this time."

"That's usually how it is nowadays," said Tyler. "Ninety percent of the time it's just some random tip-off from the Anti-Toxicity League." It was now Tyler's turn.

Mr. Zee sat behind his desk and read from a long list. "Tyler Base, senior."

"Hello again Mr. Zee," Tyler said as he sat down. His tune sounded no different to Isaiah than when he first launched the *Gates Sentinel*. "How've you been?"

Mr. Zee ignored the pleasantry. "You're accused of spreading toxic gossip. What do you have to say for yourself?"

"What else is new?"

"Don't you have any remorse for the damage you've done? Or empathy for those who heard your toxic words?"

"Which rival gossip column was it this time?"

Mr. Zee let out a deep sigh. "Are you going to apologize or not?"

Tyler shook his head. "I have nothing to apologize for."

"That's going to be two days after school," said Mr. Zee. "It could've been one, if only you'd listen."

"Whatever. "Can I go?"

"Not yet," said Mr. Zee. "You have a second offense today. You're accused of sneaking into a classroom just before the bell rang and writing 'class is cancelled' on the chalkboard. This caused two dozen freshmen to miss their midterm. What do you have to say for yourself?"

"Come on, Mr. Zee," said Tyler. "That's ridiculous. It's not even time for midterms yet."

"It was reported in the *Gates Times* this morning," Mr. Zee said, as though that settled the matter. "So what do you have to say for yourself Tyler?"

"As usual, I'm not apologizing," Tyler said, shaking his head for a second time.

"In that case, that's two days detention turned into four." Mr. Zee narrowed his eyes in stern disapproval. "As a matter of fact, tack on an extra day for your attitude. That's five days of detention - an entire school week. You will report for those detentions once you have finished serving all the time you have already accumulated."

"Well, that's a first," said Tyler.

"Just get out of here before I give you another detention. Next."

As Tyler walked out the door, Isaiah took his seat in front before Mr. Zee.

"Isaiah, senior. You're accused of spreading toxic gossip. What do you have to say for yourself?"

Isaiah took a deep breath. "I apologize. I'll say I'm sorry to whomever I hurt. I know you won't tell me who it was that complained, but whoever it was, and whatever it was I said, I apologize for it." There was no way Isaiah could tolerate a second day's detention on top of having to go through this.

"Why did you do what you did?" asked Mr. Zee.

Isaiah was taken aback. Last time Mr. Zee had just given him a single day's detention at this point. Then he was sent on his way. Today, Mr. Zee asked Isaiah a follow-up question instead. "I-I don't know, but it won't happen again."

Mr. Zee eyed him carefully. "No reduction."

Isaiah's widened his eyes in astonishment. "What?"

"No reduction," Mr. Zee repeated.

"Why not?"

"Isaiah, I understand that you wrote rival gossip columns for the *Gates Sentinel* while it was still in print. Also, you've now had multiple offenses on your record. With that in mind, I don't feel its right to let you off the hook again so easily."

"I never wrote rival gossip columns," Isaiah protested.

"Furthermore," Mr. Zee continued as if uninterrupted. "I've seen you fraternizing with unscrupulous characters such as Tyler Base. There are persistent rumors that you have been part of the smear campaign against Hallie Flynn. It's clear to me that you need to become more aware of your actions in the future. Therefore, you will serve two days in detention."

"That's not fair," said Isaiah. "I apologized." Even if he had not meant it or known what it was truly for.

"Reduction of punishment is a courtesy, Isaiah," explained Mr. Zee. "It is not guaranteed. When Principal Terrence realized what was going on he put careful consideration into our new policies regarding the toxic epidemic. Next."

Isaiah stood up and the next customer for high school jail sat in his place.

Mr. Zee turned his attention to the girl in front of him. "Erica Cairo-Mellow, sophomore."

Isaiah now felt worse. More than anything he wished he had done as Tyler had done. At least he would have his dignity. When he left the room and the door closed behind him, Isaiah played out in his head what it would have been like if he had handled it differently. If only he could take back his fruitless apology, but it was too late. Judgment had been passed.

* * *

Mr. Zee's detention room was more full every day. He no longer handled the oversight of the detention room by himself. The room was now filled up every day and typically they had to bring extra chairs in to accommodate all the "toxic" miscreants. Members of the In Crowd took turns coming to the detention room after school and standing at the front, reading the *Gates Times* to all those present.

Tyler Base went to Mr. Zee's office every day, without exception. Although he often had multiple offenses, he never once apologized and always took the two-day option. "Stay strong," he told everyone when he did this. "Never play ball with them, no matter what they tell you." In his latest underground *Gates Sentinel* articles he gave tips on how to survive on the run from Antenor, T-Bone and Farouk.

Whenever the In Crowder reading the articles came to a gossip column about someone currently in detention, they spoke loudly and glared at them as they read. Considering there was significant overlap between those in detention and those featured in the gossip columns, this happened fairly frequently.

A football player with long hair came to a gossip column about Tyler Base one day. He approached Tyler's seat and shouted every word of the article at him one at a time. Tyler merely sat back and smirked. A *Gates Times* photographer took a picture of Tyler sitting still and smirking as the yelling football player got up in his face. This picture appeared on the front page of the *Gates Times* the following day, and Tyler was given the title King of the Untouchables.

The In Crowd soon regretted this, as Tyler embraced their given nickname for him. He had a custom t-shirt made for himself which had a smiling picture of Teddy the Toad with the words "King of the Untouchables" beneath it. Tyler started wearing this shirt to school every day, and every day he was scolded for it and given another two afternoons of detention. Undeterred, he continued with his moral support to those who were also labeled Untouchable. That, along with his underground publishing of the *Gates Sentinel*, continued to earn him even more detentions.

Chapter 18: Halloween Pranks

Despite widespread belief that the present crazes would die down sooner or later, nothing ceased in the seemingly-never-ending escalation between those claiming to be fighting "toxicity" and those defending the Out Crowd from the In Crowd. A few dozen students who the *Gates Times* had targeted in their gossip columns found their houses toilet-papered or egged in the latter half of October. Karen's house was egged after a gossip column was run about her past relationships with Isaiah and any lingering toxic karma she might have leftover from her past interactions with him.

Pranks started going in both directions. Hallie's house was egged shortly before Halloween and the school security guards interviewed Hallie after homeroom so they could look into the matter further. Even if the incident in question occurred off of school grounds, they said, some discipline on the matter might be required. Just as Hallie Flynn had wrapped up her interview with the security guards, her fellow senior Karen happened to be passing by.

Hallie strut down the hall in her cheerleading uniform with both pom-poms dangling from her backpack like a keychain. She was flanked by a junior cheerleader on one side and a sophomore cheerleader on the other.

"Excuse me." Karen approached the security guards. She tucked her cell phone into her pocket and gave them her full attention. "My house was also egged the other night. Do you have a minute? I can give you the details."

The pair of security guards reacted differently. One of them grunted and looked away. The second was more cordial. "Sorry," he told her politely, but firmly. "At this time we're only interested in the egging of Hallie Flynn's house."

* * *

Near the end of October, Gates High School held its annual Halloween Parade. This was one the third most anticipated regular events of the Gates school calendar besides Prom and Homecoming. It always occurred on one of the days in the week preceding Halloween, though the actual day and time varied based on other factors of the school schedule. As usual, all the kids were looking forward to it. This year it also represented a chance to get their mind off of other things.

It was held on Monday of the week before Halloween, but there was a problem. Almost no one knew it was that day in advance because there was no public announcement. This did not prevent any of the In Crowd from being in the know. Only a handful of lucky Out Crowders heard from other sources or told their friends. Since the *Gates Times*, the only remaining school publication, solely ran gossip columns these days, nothing was in the paper. Usually there would have been an announcement in homeroom, but homeroom now consisted of everyone being handed copies of the *Gates Times* and being given some quiet time to read it.

Therefore, on the day of the Halloween Parade, about ten percent of the students came dressed in costumes. The rest wore ordinary clothes because they didn't realize the parade was that day. Joel Boudin dressed up as a zombie. Hallie Flynn came to school in her cheerleading uniform and drenched herself in fake blood. This symbolized all the pain and suffering she had endured throughout the year. Shelly Boudin took it upon herself to snap a picture of Hallie with the streams of red running down her body. Hallie was promptly declared the winner of the GHS costume contest, before any of the other entries could be looked at or considered.

Some Out Crowders who aligned with the In Crowd clapped for her. Hallie gave a short nod of approval to each of them. This was far less of a reward than sitting with the In Crowd for lunch, but a somber Hallie was no longer in as giving a mood as she had been in the weeks preceding.

Just like every other year, the Halloween Parade started at the visitor center lobby and progressed through all seven wings of the school. It went on for almost an hour and this year that hour dragged on longer than ever.

"This is so lame and embarrassing," Isaiah said to Craig and Karen. "Doing this whole costume parade with no costumes."

"You and everyone else, Isaiah," Craig told him.

Two sophomore boys managed to find out about the parade from overhearing one of the English teachers speaking to Principal Terrence about it. They were among the few lucky members of the Out Crowd who knew to dress up. One of them came as Teddy the Toad and the other as one of the Crying Kitties. Both of them put some dirt on their noses like they had just done the Splat. Right after the parade ended, a pair of In Crowd girls caught a glimpse of them and began shrieking like harpies.

Mrs. Friedman rushed to the scene as soon as she heard them. She suspended both sophomore boys without asking for any of the specifics of the situation, but reminded them that they were still expected to attend football games even while suspended (expulsions were still on hold until after the football season).

Seemingly satisfied, the two cheerleaders ceased their harpy-like screaming. Appropriately perhaps, they were both wearing harpy costumes.

"I wish I thought to do something like that," said Isaiah.

Karen raised her eyebrow. "You've kidding, right?"

"I'm half serious," he said simply.

"I don't entirely blame you Isaiah," said Craig. "Pretty much nobody enjoyed this. Most anticlimactic parade ever." The Halloween Parades during their freshman, sophomore and junior years had all been fabulous.

"Everett didn't have fun either," Karen pointed out. "He looked depressed."

"Yeah he did," agreed Craig. "I was gonna approach him, but he looked away as soon as he saw me." Apparently no one in the Out Crowd enjoyed the so-called Halloween Parade.

"I forgot my application form for the Jefferson Lee scholarship fund the other day," Isaiah said. "I had to run home and get it. As soon as I did, I had to rush back to school before I was caught." Luckily no one seemed to notice him leaving or returning. The school security guards were too busy monitoring for toxic behavior. "I was so stressed out I forgot to go to detention yesterday. I got an extra day because of that."

"That sucks," said Karen. "So do you have two days of detention in a row now?"

Isaiah shook his head. "Three. I already had two."

"Is it true you can't use your cell phone while you're in detention?" Karen asked, as though nothing could be crueler.

"Yes," said Isaiah.

"That must stink," said Karen. "My house got egged over the weekend. I don't know which was worse. That or today's parade."

Isaiah felt his blood begin to boil. "All because you stood up for a nice guy who tutored you last year."

"Twice I tried to report it to the school," said Karen. "They told me to watch my words about the In Crowd and not to incite anything else."

Isaiah was furious. "You weren't inciting anything against the In Crowd!"

"No, she didn't," said Craig. "She didn't say anything mean about anyone. She just said something nice about a guy who wrote for a publication the In Crowd hates about a play he didn't like."

"He didn't even say he hated it," said Isaiah. "That was Marian Jay. His review was neutral."

"True," said Craig. "But Jimmy Hugo is the In Crowd's favorite Out Crowder. That play was like a sacred cow for them."

"I see." Isaiah digested this. Regardless of what he had seen these past several weeks something the next day always surprised him even more. "The lesson of the day is simple then. We all know how to not be toxic now."

Karen exchanged a glance with Craig. "How?" she asked Isaiah.

"Don't say anything or do anything."

* * *

The days after the nearly costumeless costume parade, the *Gates Times* published the picture of Hallie covered in blood and ran a few gossip columns speculating on who may have egged her house. Those suspects had their houses toilet-papered that evening. Principal Terrence convened another sensitivity assembly and said that while he could not condone toilet-papering houses, that he could not help but feel proud of whoever had done the retaliatory act in Hallie's honor.

Senior cheerleader Tammy White was brought up in the following issue of the *Gates Times*. Tammy was easily one of the most forgettable members of the In Crowd. She had challenged Hallie for the position of captain at the end of their junior year. Hallie Flynn defeated Tammy White handily and the latter was soon forgotten. Tammy briefly came back into the limelight when her house got egged. The *Gates Times* theorized in a gossip column that whomever had egged Hallie's house may also have egged Tammy's. Soon, however, it was discovered that Tammy had in fact egged her own house. With that, she was immediately forgotten again.

After school, Isaiah saw he had a voicemail. "Hello Isaiah. This is Mr. De Moore calling again from the Jefferson Lee Scholarship Fund. Hope all is well. Listen; regarding your application to our program, there's been a development. I know when we last spoke I told you that you would be awarded a Jefferson Lee Scholarship for next year. Since then a representative of the Anti-Toxicity League from Gates High School has reached out to us and informed me that you have been classified as Untouchable. I wasn't familiar with that distinction, but the rep explained to me that it rendered the recommendation letters we received null and void. I'm not sure why that's the case but apparently it's official policy now. As you know, each applicant to our program is required to have two letters of recommendation from their teachers in order to qualify. Because those letters are now void, your spot in our program is likewise rescinded. This was not a decision we made on our own, but the Anti-Toxicity League has communicated this development to us and now I am communicating it to you. Best of luck to you on your future endeavors."

Chapter 19: Crisis and Crisis Again

A new panic descended on Gates High. Tyler Base was now maxed out on detention, quite literally. While it was only early November, Tyler was now scheduled for detention every day after school through graduation in June. The tough question arose of what to do with him on further offenses. Summer school may have been an option, but Tyler was a senior and giving anyone detention or punishment after they had already graduated was impossible.

The *Gates Times* wrote frantic articles confronting the possibility that Tyler may be able to get away with being as toxic as he wanted from now on with no further consequences. This was something that neither the In Crowd nor their allies could bear. One of the members of the Anti-Toxicity League said that he saw something called "Saturday detention" in a movie and suggested giving that to Tyler. It would only delay the inevitable a little while longer. At the rate he was going, Tyler would get be booked for detention every Saturday of the year soon enough, but at least it would buy time to think of other options.

Unfortunately for the Anti-Toxicity League, Principal Terrence quickly shot the idea down. "That would make sense for this situation," he explained, "but reluctantly I must say that

Gates High doesn't have any policy providing for Saturday detention, so that's not going to be an option for us."

Others suggested extending the hours of detention, but Mr. Zee refused to stay after school any longer than he already was. Before this year he had not even had to oversee detention every day, since there were plenty of days where nobody was in detention. With this no longer being the case, Mr. Zee was unwilling to volunteer any additional time after school. No other teacher was willing to do so in his stead, either.

Lunch detention was another option that was brought up. At the current pace, however, Tyler Base would also max out on lunch detention sometime in January.

"I think I might be labeled as Untouchable soon," Karen said one day at lunch. She was sitting with Isaiah and Craig. The girls Karen normally sat with had evicted her from her former table. Now she sat in Everett's former seat, which he had self-evicted from.

Isaiah laughed humorlessly. "Welcome to the club." He had been informed of his new status by the Anti-Toxicity League right after his scholarship got rescinded.

Karen sighed deeply. "Everything's gotten so out of hand this year," she said.

"Yes, it has," agreed Craig.

"How did this happen?" she wondered aloud. She twisted the spaghetti on her tray with her plastic fork, but didn't eat any. "Hallie, and Joel, and Tyler Base. They've all ruined everything by gossiping too much." She and Craig shared a nod.

"Tyler's different," said Isaiah. "He had the right intentions. Somebody had to fight back against Hallie and Joel."

MICHAEL A. KIRBY

"Tyler's an impulsive show-off," Craig said, shaking his head. "If we lived in a saner school he wouldn't be as popular."

"Exactly," said Isaiah. "He doesn't allow himself to get pushed around by the In Crowd, he never apologizes and he inspires the Out Crowd." Truthfully, Isaiah would have started taking Tyler Base's attitude long ago if it weren't far outside his usual comfort zone.

Craig stopped chewing and put his hands up. "I get it, okay. I just wish there were someone else standing up to Hallie and Joel and it wasn't just him."

Karen shrugged. "Honestly Isaiah, I'm more impressed with your approach than his. Just trying to be reasonable and getting along with everyone."

"This is serious Karen," said Isaiah.

"I'm being serious," she said with a faint trace of a smile. "You don't need to rely on Tyler."

Isaiah was taken aback. "Well Tyler knows it's not all about him. He has a point to prove and that's why he won't stop doing what he's doing."

"What point is that?" asked Craig.

"That it's okay to be part of the Out Crowd."

Craig stopped chewing. Frantically, he spun about to make sure no one was listening to their conversation, then he turned back to his friends. "Isaiah, you shouldn't say things like that," he whispered. "That sounds really toxic."

Isaiah was undaunted. "Why?" he asked Craig. "Why is that toxic?"

Craig scratched his head. "Ummm...well…"

"Look," said Isaiah. "Even if the In Crowd says that's toxic, it shouldn't be."

Craig calmed down and thought for a second. "You're right. It shouldn't be."

At any rate, no one was able to resolve the dilemma about Tyler Base before another crisis surfaced. The league commissioner for Western County high school sports had sent a notice to Coach Ericks concerning the team and the upcoming county finals where Gates' football team would compete against Byzantine High.

"It has come to my attention," the letter read, "that three of your players are below the minimum academic standards for competition." He was referring to Antenor, T-Bone and Farouk. "All student athletes competing in county-wide events must maintain a C average to be eligible." Countywide policy dictated that every competitor must have a C average to play. Some individual schools had a higher standard as a school policy. Gates itself, like the rest of these schools, required their players to get a Bs. Then there was Oxford High School, which required its student athletes to all have straight As. Regardless, all three of the students in question were far beneath any of those standards. The league commissioner threatened Gates High School with immediate disqualification if any of the three players in question set foot on the field during the finals.

Farouk's parents resumed talks about sending their son to military school.

"This is beyond unfair," Hallie said to Shelly at lunch. With Antenor, T-Bone and Farouk gone, they would lose three trusted allies in the war against toxicity. "I'm so depressed. We should write a gossip column about the league commissioner!"

"We can't do that," said Shelly. "He's an adult."

"Oh please," Hallie retorted. "It's not like he's a teacher or anything."

"Exactly," said Shelly. "So he probably doesn't care one way or the other what kids at our school say about him. Face it Hallie, we've taken this as far as we can, and now it's over. We lost."

"No, it can't be," said Hallie. "I still have one more card up my sleeve...I think. God, this breaks my heart." She cried as she hugged Shelly Boudin, who patted her awkwardly on the back.

Principal Terrence came by just as they released each other. When Hallie caught his eye, he stopped by their table. "Right, so I saw the news about the league commissioner," he said, averting his gaze. "Most unfortunate."

"You're the principal," said Hallie, her eyes still watering. "Can't you do something?"

"I'm afraid not," Principal Terrence said. "The league commissioner is beyond my reach."

Hallie cried out in anger. "You're useless!" she snapped at him. "Get out of my sight!"

Principal Terrence hung his head and walked back to his office in shame.

"Tyler's probably thrilled at this news," Hallie said, glancing across the cafeteria at him. "He's got that shirt on again. I can't believe he wears it every day. It must really stink by now."

"No it doesn't," Shelly said before she could stop herself. "He must have multiple of the same shirt."

"What? How do you know that?"

Shelly looked away. "I've passed him in the hall a few times."

Hallie shrugged it off. "Whatever. Anyhow, things are pretty bad right now, so we have to remain vigilant." The captain of the cheerleading squad gawked at the Editor of the *Gates Times*. "Shelly, are you blushing!?"

"What? No!" Her cheeks, however, were bright red and she wasted no time in averting her gaze. "Say, Hallie, did we ever find out who was being toxic?"

"Huh?" Hallie Flynn looked confused. "What are you talking about Shelly? We've exposed lots of toxic people in our teamwork together. The Untouchables section of your paper is littered with them."

"I know," said Shelly. "But what about right after Brett Webster's blog?"

"What does any of this have to do with Brett? I am so over him," Hallie said irritably. "And he doesn't even go here anymore."

"Over the summer he posted that blog people gossiped about," said Shelly. "Remember?"

"So what? That's yesterday's news. In fact, that's way beyond yesterday's news at this point," said Hallie. "Thanks for reminding me," she added sarcastically.

"My point is...I don't think we ever actually found out who was gossiping about that blog," said Shelly. "The original toxic people. Didn't you say Jarvis initially convinced you to resist the toxic environment at Gates because of them?"

"Huh," said Hallie. "Jarvis?"

"When you were eating pizza with the rest of the In Crowd. Shortly before you came to me and we started the gossip columns. What started...well, everything. Don't you remember?"

"Oh yeah, him. Honestly, Jarvis isn't the most memorable of football players. Anyway, who cares if there were toxic people then? There are obviously toxic people now."

"Yes," said Shelly. She scanned the cafeteria. With her experience in journalistic investigation, Shelly was able to decipher at first glance what many of her fellow students were thinking. Some, like Hallie Flynn, were moping about the possibility of Antenor, T-Bone and Farouk leaving for good and opening the door to exponential increases in toxicity. Others were biting their lips, almost as if they were secretly happy but were doing their best to hide it. Disturbingly, Shelly could not shake the impression that the number of lib-biters had grown over time while the number of mopers had shrunk. "There are."

"Toxic people just can't stop being toxic," Hallie said matter-of-factly. "Just means there's more work for us to do."

"All our work," Shelly thought out loud, "over all these gossip cycles. What have we actually accomplished?"

"You look tired Shelly," said Hallie. "Have a cup of coffee before you get to work on the next issue."

"The next issue," said Shelly, barely paying attention. "Right."

* * *

That evening, the league commissioner made an announcement on local public access. "Good evening, everyone," he began. The league commissioner's voice sounded rehearsed. "I have something that I need to say to the people of Western County, regarding our interschool football competitions. Good news and bad news. Let's start with the bad. As most of you know, we have a rule in our league that for anyone to be eligible to compete they must meet required academic standard. This rule has not changed and we're still as stringent about it as we have been in the past. However, recently the league has suffered an…um…lack of…um…resources. Yes, a lack of resources, let's go with that. Thus, we are unable to enforce this rule on our own. Instead we will rely on every individual school to enforce this regulation as it applies to their own players.

"We will be relying on their cooperation completely. In the mean time, the league will not investigate any individual student's academic performance, nor will we respond to any complaint about an individual student failing to meet the academic standard. All such complaints will be directed to the principals of whatever school those students attend, who will have full autonomy in the enforcement of this policy, at least until the end of this season. That's the bad news."

The league commissioner took a deep breath. "Let's move onto the good news. Our organization recently signed a contract to have all our football games televised on local TV stations across Western County. Furthermore, spectator seating is getting upgraded and college referees who have overseen games at Big City University will referee our games. You heard me right. We will have college referees at our high school football games, on top of televised games and every field will have an upgraded venue, with turf included.

"Some of you may be wondering how this is all possible when I just said earlier that the league is undergoing a lack of resources. Well, this is all made possible from a very generous donation we have just received tonight. That *very* generous donor behind it is none other than Harold Flynn, founder and CEO of Flynn Telecommunications. I heard from an inside source that Mr. Flynn was responsible for partial renovations for the football field at his own town's high school earlier in the year. His daughter is apparently the captain of the cheerleading squad there.

"In honor of this very generous donation, the Western County High School Football Championship will henceforth be renamed the Flynn Bowl. The inaugural Flynn Bowl will be held this weekend at Gates High School, as they go head to head with Byzantine High School."

Chapter 20: The Flynn Bowl

On the day of the Flynn Bowl, preparations were made for a football game unlike any ever seen at Gates High School before. A concession stand was hired on. The bleachers were expanded up a few more levels – the second time such an expansion had taken place in this school year alone. During the early hours of the morning, technicians had arrived to upgrade the lighting system for games that played into the evening. Since kickoff time was in the early afternoon, these would probably not be required for today. Then again, if Hallie and Joel kept lengthening their dances perhaps the first Flynn Bowl would last into the evening. The visitor's section of the audience was not nearly as large as the one for the home team. After all, Byzantine High did not have a policy requiring everyone enrolled as a student there to attend their football games. No other school in Western County did. Only Gates. Several employees from Flynn Telecommunications polished the scoreboard and spruced up the field.

Wooden construction frames were erected around the field to build a stadium. The construction itself was not scheduled to begin until December. Nevertheless, the foreman had mapped out the foundations and fenced off the necessary areas in advance. Because of this, the field was only accessible from two entrances: the regular entrance between the concrete pillars and a smaller side entrance used by the workers and security guards.

When combined together, the expensive renovations amounted to a project that would take multiple days if not weeks. Mr. Flynn brought in over a hundred workers who completed everything except for the stadium construction in a single morning.

There was also added security. Every security guard currently employed by Gates High was stationed on the football field for the Flynn Bowl. The security guards visited student's houses in the morning to remind them of the game. As the crowd gathered and kick-off time approached, the security guards garrisoned themselves around the field. Antenor, T-Bone and Farouk assisted the security guards in patrolling the field's perimeters while the rest of the Gates team warmed up. Antenor took the north side, T-Bone took the south side and Farouk guarded the small area between the outer fence and the spot where Hallie Flynn and the rest of the cheerleaders were doing their own warm-up stretches.

Byzantine High School's team was warming up next to the goal post opposite from Gates' end. Evan Terrence had clearly trained hard before today. Byzantine was now favored, despite losing their earlier game against Gates. They had lost no other games while Gates had lost two over the course of the season. Byzantine High School was unchanged, but Gates High School was unrecognizable from Homecoming ten weeks prior.

The senior members of the Out Crowd were given priority for the closest seats to the field, with the juniors, sophomores and freshmen behind them, respectively. That is, except for the Untouchables, who were given seats at the top of the bleachers, regardless of their grade.

On his way up to the Untouchables section, Isaiah noticed Dan from Dungeons and Dragons Club sitting next to a former smoker. That smoker used to bully Dan and take his lunch money. Today, however, the two new friends wore matching scowls as everybody waited for the game to start. Normally, such a turn of events would have made Isaiah more curious, but in the past few months that was the least of the unusual developments. Naturally, Tyler Base was also up there, wearing his "King of the Untouchables" shirt. He looked comfortably at home compared to the rest of his companions.

"Hey Isaiah," Karen said as she sat down next to him.

Isaiah was surprised. "Karen? Were you labeled Untouchable already?"

"Just this morning," she said, shrugging it off as though it didn't matter. "The *Gates Times* finally mentioned me in one gossip column too many."

"Hello," Craig greeted as he joined them both.

"Are you sure you should be here Craig?" Karen asked.

"She's got a point, Craig," said Isaiah. "You're not Untouchable. You've never even been in a gossip column. That could change if you sit here with us voluntarily."

"Meh, it's only a matter of time before I'm told to come here anyway," Craig waved this statement away. "It's only a matter of time before we're all told to come here."

"Why are you so dressed up?" Isaiah saw that Craig was wearing a suit and tie to the Flynn Bowl. Because of this, Craig's entire tattoo was concealed, save for a couple branches and half of the infinity symbol.

"My family and I were visiting my grandma this morning," Craig answered as he sat down. "She's terminally ill."

"I'm sorry to hear that, dude," said Isaiah. "Please let me know if there's anything that I can do."

"Mom said it would be nice if everyone looked their best," said Craig. "About ten minutes after we got there one of the school security guards swung by to pick me up and take me to the game."

"How did they even know where to find you?" asked Karen.

"I think someone from the Anti-Toxicity League overheard me talking about it in homeroom," said Craig.

"This is going to be a long day," moaned Karen.

"I know," Craig agreed in despair. "I can't believe we're forced to sit here and endure four entire quarters of this."

Once everyone had enough time to get to their seats, the kickoff began. Gates won the coin toss, so Byzantine High School kicked and Joel Boudin caught the ball. Joel dodged and swerved back and forth to evade the Byzantine tacklers, though he made more of a show of it than necessary. When the play finally ended he was tackled at the fifty-one yard line.

The seniors in the front row who had bought coffee from the concession stand soon regretted it. Bathroom breaks were only permitted in between quarters.

"Well, we're all here again," Isaiah said to Karen and Craig, but mostly to himself.

"We didn't want to come," said Craig.

"But they made us," Karen said about the In Crowd. She was just as resigned as Isaiah and Craig were.

"Right," said Isaiah. "They told us we had to, and we came." Suddenly, he felt alert. It was as if Isaiah had remembered something that he and everyone else around him had forgotten. "The only reason they have power over us is...we give it to them."

"Huh?" said Craig.

"The only reason that the In Crowd can control the Out Crowd is we allow them to," said Isaiah. "If you take everything that shouldn't matter out of the equation, they're a group of kids just like the Out Crowd." His alertness spread from his head to the rest of him. "A much smaller group." Intensity coursed through Isaiah's pulsating veins, and with it came the urge to do something drastic and unheard of.

"I guess so," said Karen. "But what can we do Isaiah?"

"There's nothing we can do," said Craig.

"Yes there is," Isaiah said as he stood up. "We can walk away."

"What?" said Craig; unsure he had heard his friend right. "Just leave the game?"

"Yes," said Isaiah. "Let's just walk away and leave all this behind. Walk away from the game. Walk away from this mess. Walk away from the In Crowd."

"Are you nuts?" said Karen. "We're *required* to be at this game. Do you know what the consequences would be if we just left?"

"I do not," Isaiah admitted. "But I don't care anymore. I'm done with worrying about what the consequences will be. I'm walking away. I don't ask you to follow if you don't want to."

"He's nuts," said Craig.

"Yeah," said Karen, smirking. "He is." She got to her feet and began walking down the bleachers after Isaiah.

Craig sighed. "I guess that we are, too." He followed suit.

Murmurs came with each new step that Isaiah, Karen and Craig took.

"What are they doing?"

"Are they leaving?"

"No, they can't be. They must be changing seats."

"It doesn't look like they're changing seats."

"They just left the Untouchables section. I think they're planning to leave the field." Half a dozen other Untouchables joined the walking away soon after Isaiah, Karen and Craig stood up. All the convincing they had needed was for someone else to do it first.

"That boy in front said they were walking away from the game. I heard him."

"Should we walk away?"

"Are we allowed to?"

"No."

"We're not allowed to, but can we get away with it?"

"I don't know, but they're trying. If we follow them, maybe we'll all have a chance."

The walking away line swelled to include the entire Untouchables section. Some members of the other four sections were more reluctant at first, but they also joined in one by one.

"Won't we get detention?" Angie the smoker wondered aloud.

"Who cares at this point?" Brad the smoker said as he stood up. "Let's go." Brad stared back at Angie, who nodded in agreement and followed.

"Wow," Craig said in amazement. "Look behind you Isaiah." There was a long and growing line of Out Crowders in their trail. "You started this."

Plump and pimply Sally Smith also joined the walk away. She strutted down the bleachers slowly, holding both her bulky arms out for balance. Behind Sally were Yazidi, the new girl and Roy Wilson, the subject of many early gossip columns. Behind them were Dan from Dungeons and Dragons Club and his smoker companion. Even sophomores Anna Mason and Gary Jackson, frequent interviewees for the *Gates Times* over the past couple months, both decided to join in.

Hallie Flynn was standing atop her cheerleading pyramid when the departing Out Crowders caught her eye. She immediately lost her balance and fell down ten feet. Each of her fellow cheerleaders holding her up also lost their balance and tumbled over at the same time their captain hit the ground. As Hallie got back up, she wiped the mud off her face, eyes blazing and chest heaving.

"What are they doing?" she said in sheer disbelief. "They can't leave…and yet they are." As though electrified, Hallie sprang up and ran outside the inner fence and approached the lead security guard, who was next to the concession stand scarfing down a hot dog. "Look," she told him, pointing. "They're leaving."

The lead security guard shrugged it off. "I think you're mistaken. They must be changing seats."

Hallie gawked at him. "All of them at once? I don't think so."

"Then they must be sneaking out to pee," he replied. "They'll be back. Football attendance is mandated and this is well known. They're required to stay."

"I know that," snapped Hallie. "They're leaving the game anyway. Do something about it."

The lead security guard sighed as he brushed the crumbs off his uniform. "Fine, Hallie," he relented. "What are your orders?"

"Secure the perimeter," the cheerleading captain instructed the lead security guard. "Don't let anyone from the bleachers exit the premises."

Isaiah, Karen and Craig led the rest of the Out Crowd and reached the concrete pathways. Now that they were out of the seating area, however, it became clear that walking away from the game was easier said than done.

They could not cross the field because there was no way around it. By the time they were in front of the main entrance, the security guards were already in place. A few kids from the herd broke away from Isaiah and the others. They tried climbing the fences, but the lead security guard saw them at once. He directed the other GHS security guards to shake the fences and every teenager fell off before reaching the other side.

Hallie ran onto the football field in the middle of a play to confront a very confused Joel. No sooner had she pointed him to the Out Crowders walking away than he hustled off the field, taking the rest of the Gates High School team with him.

The referee from Big City University shouted something very loud that no one paid attention to, about this not being a legitimate excuse to stop a game. Gates High fumbled the ball and Byzantine High School's team picked it up and scored a touchdown. They made the field goal to score the extra point, did an onside kick toward an empty field, recovered the ball and scored another touchdown. Gates was now losing fourteen to zero. A disastrous beginning, but the In Crowd had other things to worry about.

"Ninety percent of the school is about to become Untouchable," said Isaiah. "I think I've gotten myself expelled." A couple weeks ago Isaiah would have considered it a disaster just to lose his Jefferson Lee scholarship.

"No," said Craig. "We're all getting ourselves expelled. Let's do it in the best way possible.

Isaiah shook his head. "Maybe this was a bad idea. I regret dragging others along."

"You don't have a right to feel that way," Karen told him sharply. She was more blunt with Isaiah than she had been since he forgot her birthday when they were both juniors. "You're not dragging anyone to do anything. Don't think like the In Crowd, Isaiah. We're all doing this voluntarily, just as much as you. Did you have any regret when you thought only you were getting in trouble? No, because you made that decision for yourself. Well, so did me and Craig, and everyone else in the Out Crowd. Give us some credit. We're all in this together, so don't start doubting what you've done now."

"Hmmm." Isaiah considered this. "Well in that case, let's get out of here."

This was still a difficult task. A horde of security guards lined the area. The bleachers on either side formed long barriers. The In Crowders were now standing between the concrete pillars of the main entrance, which was also the only clear exit. Isaiah thought. Now that he had started the walk away, he had to see it through. Otherwise it would all be for nothing and the rest of the Out Crowd would pay the price alongside him. "We can't go that way," he announced. "Let's try to find another way out."

"There's still the side entrance," said Craig. "We could try that." When they reached it, however, they found the door in the wooden frame was also closed off. There was an unusual-looking lock holding it closed.

"What's this?" Isaiah said. The lock was electronic. "I don't think that can be picked or broken." He looked back up at the bleachers. By now everyone in the Out Crowd had stood up and were gradually spilling onto the pathway. They were looking in the direction of Isaiah, Craig and Karen for what to do next. Isaiah would be partly to blame if he got all their hopes up for nothing.

Karen nudged Isaiah aside. "Let me take a look," she said. "I've seen a lock like this before. If you open it up, you can disable it."

"Great," said Craig, a note of urgency rising in his voice. He seemed to be thinking along the same lines as Isaiah. "Can you do it?"

"I forget how," said Karen. "It requires doing something with the wires inside, but it's possible." She reached into her pocket and took out her phone. "I've seen it in an online video. I'll pull it up on my phone. It's only a couple minutes long."

"Ugh," said Isaiah. "Hurry up." A couple minutes sounded like way too much time to him now, but there was no other choice. "Craig, let's each run and check for other ways out. I'll check this end of the pathway and you check the farther one." Isaiah didn't think there were any, but it helped to have a Plan B.

"Got it," Craig concurred. He sprinted off faster than Isaiah had ever seen him run before.

"Huh," Isaiah mumbled under his breath. "Perhaps Craig should've tried out for football."

None of the security guards saw what Karen was up to yet. They were still closely watching the main entranceway. Every member of the In Crowd locked arms in front of the gateway to exit the field, blocking escape route. Some students tried pushing up against them, but the football players and cheerleaders held their line firm. They kicked away anyone who tried crawling between their bodies, so none of their fellow Gates High Schoolers could leave the Flynn Bowl. The Out Crowd dispersed and looked in different directions. While they all to walk away, none of them wanted to walk through Antenor, T-Bone and Farouk, who joined Hallie Flynn and Joel Boudin's impenetrable human barrier.

Hallie tapped Joel on the shoulder. "Look over there." She was pointing at Karen. "Kelly, or what's-her-name. Phone girl. She's up to something, Joel. Go stop her."

"I'm on it, Hallie," said Joel. He dashed towards Karen.

When Isaiah looked back again, his insides froze. Karen was just finishing watching her lock-picking video, but she didn't see Joel Boudin running toward her, his lip curling. Isaiah didn't think twice before doubling back and shoving himself at Joel seconds before Joel would have collided with Karen.

In the middle of hacking the lock, Karen turned around to see what the crash behind her had been. "Wow," she said, shocked. "Thanks Isaiah."

"Don't mention it," said Isaiah, just regaining his balance. Any relief Isaiah had did not last. He had physically confronted Joel Boudin, who was much larger than he was. Isaiah had managed to catch him off guard, but Joel was not caught by surprise anymore. Towering over Isaiah, Joel had never been more ferocious to behold. But just as Joel was about to pounce on Isaiah, he was knocked out of the way again...this time by a freshman shorter even than Isaiah. Then a second underclassman bumped into Joel. And a third. And a fourth. And so on. Isaiah still couldn't believe he had charged at Joel Boudin himself moments before. Now a pack of fearless underclassmen were swarming their senior captain and pinning him to the ground. There were at least twenty freshmen and sophomores piling on top of him at once. Joel Boudin stood no chance against all of them together.

Back on the football field, Evan Terrence from Byzantine High School watched from a distance. He howled with laughter as Gates High School's own spectators tackled his rival.

Hallie Flynn hurried over, bringing several other In Crowders with her. "Oh that's nice," she said sarcastically, addressing the underclassmen who held down Joel Boudin. "Real nice. Tackle your own star player. Do Byzantine High School's work for them."

As Karen finally unlocked up the side door, Hallie dove in front and cut her off. She locked arms with Antenor, T-Bone, Farouk and half a dozen other In Crowders to form a second human barrier in front of the side entrance. They had acted just in time, since the remaining Out Crowders had all begun marching toward the side entrance. "Stop it, you toxic Byzantine conspirators!" Hallie shouted. "Go back to your seats."

"We're leaving today whether you like it or not," Isaiah said to Hallie. There was no turning back. Isaiah could never apologize his way out of this action even if he wanted to. His comfort zone no longer existed. Now that he couldn't go back into his bubble, he had no reason not to confront the In Crowd as directly as possible.

Hallie scoffed. "That's cute. Do you really think I'll let any of you be toxic and miss the game?"

"What game?" said Isaiah. "You already abandoned the game yourself, Hallie. Don't talk to us about a game. You can't fool us anymore." This was Isaiah's second conversation with Hallie Flynn in their high school lives. The first one had been two years prior, when they were sophomores. He had asked her what time it was and she had said she didn't know. This conversation was already longer and much more meaningful.

"Isaiah, isn't it?" said Hallie Flynn. "None of you are going anywhere. We won't let you."

"We're not asking for permission," said Isaiah. He gestured behind him to the rest of the Out Crowd, all of whom had left their seats by now.

One lurking security guard made his way to the side entrance. He was a cop in his full-time occupation and today he made it his personal goal to stop the walking away single-handedly. He whipped out his Taser and jammed it into Dan from Dungeons and Dragons Club. Dan shook violently and then collapsed, but his smoker buddy caught his fall and hoisted him up with his shoulder. Craig had just returned, and he and the smoker balanced Dan between them.

This did not halt anything. Quite the opposite, in fact. The walk away broke into a run away. The security guard swung his arm about sticking his Taser into as many Out Crowd kids as he could, but there were too many for him to stop at once. Each time somebody collapsed to the ground, the kid behind him or her always picked them up and kept running.

"Hold the line!" Hallie called out in desperation, locking arms tighter with the linebacker on her left and the cheerleader on her right. Hallie planted both her feet firmly as Out Crowders pushed against her and her friends with tremendous force.

"I'm trying," the linebacker replied through gritted teeth. Just then he noticed that their blocking line had gotten shorter. Antenor, T-Bone and Farouk had abandoned their positions and were running away towards the woods as fast as their legs would carry them. Three puddles of urine marked where they had stood moments before. Apparently Antenor, T-Bone and Farouk were not willing to stand up to the entire Out Crowd at once.

Once the three intimidating henchmen were gone, the rest of the In Crowders in Hallie's second human barrier tumbled to the ground. The running Out Crowders trampled over them in a massive stampede. The tide of Out Crowders stormed to the edge of the Gates High School campus. The Flynn Bowl had reminded the In Crowd of the same inconvenient but unavoidable fact that had become clear on the day Class Clown was first voted on. The Out Crowd outnumbered them. At long last, the In Crowd had run out of ways to hide that.

Among the In Crowders of the second barrier, only Hallie Flynn herself was still on her feet. "Stop," she called at the fleeing mass. "Come back here this instant or I'll make all of you pay!"

Isaiah faced her again. "We were your fans," he yelled. "We looked up to you, but then you turned on us! No, Hallie. This is done." With that, he ran to catch up with the rest of the Out Crowd who had walked away with him.

Falling to her knees, Hallie was left by herself at last. "Please don't go," she whimpered, tears flowing down from her eyes. "Please. I am *nothing* without all of you…"

Everett came over to stand where Isaiah had been seconds before. He was the only member of the Out Crowd still present, with the exception of Tyler Base, who was below the bleachers making out with Shelly Boudin. Mouth-open, Everett stared at Hallie wordlessly. He had gone to school with her since kindergarten, but never had she appeared smaller to him than she did today. The other Out Crowders were now far in the distance. Finally, without saying a word, Everett also turned and departed after them.

Small shards of snow fell from the sky. This was remarkably early in the year for them to make their debut. The pieces of snow danced in the wind about Hallie. After they finished fluttering about, they trickled to the ground, and then they melted.

* * *

Hundreds of silent teenagers walked through the parking lot and toward the boundaries of the school campus. The Out Crowd was solemn and relieved at the same time. Craig hurried through the pack, squeezing between each boy and girl in front of him, until he caught up to his friends. Isaiah and Karen walked arm-in-arm together and she rested her head on his shoulder. Neither they, nor anyone else in the Out Crowd said a word at first.

"What do we even do now?" asked Karen, finally breaking the silence. "Our entire world as we know it is gone."

Isaiah was not worried. "I guess we'll have to build a new one, then."

Acknowledgements

Firstly, I would like to thank my family. As long as I can remember my parents were both helpful in my writing ambitions. They and also my brother and sister enabled me to foster my imagination, but also kept me grounded to the real world at times.

I would also like to thank the various writing teachers I have had over the years. My earliest mentors were in school as I came of age and some of my best influences later on came from friendships and online communities. Most recently I engaged with the Gotham Institute in New York City. With their professional experience the vast fog of the writing world melted away and became clear.

Particularly, I would like to thank my book doctor from Gotham. It was her trained eyes, which showed me how to breathe life into a chaotic high school environment, and also to manage the progression in the most appropriate manner. With her guidance, I finally discovered how to take The Out Crowd in the direction I wanted to from the beginning.

Next, I would like to thank John Woolf of Relics Comics, for his captivating illustrations.

Last but not least, I would like to thank my friend Josh. Without the long conversations we've had over the past few years I never would have been as inspired to take on this project as I have been. Adults, after all, are overgrown high schoolers with a little more life experience.

I am truly grateful for all the encouragement and help I have received.

Michael A. Kirby

About the Author

Ever since childhood, Michael has had a constant urge to liberate stories from the realm of his imagination and share them with the world. Various tales and characters would nag at him from inside his head until he finally agreed to give them a new life by putting pen-to-paper or finger-to-keyboard. In time, he realized this meant becoming a writer. He lives in New England, practicing yoga and drinking yerba mate on a daily basis.

Thanks for reading The Out Crowd. If you enjoyed this book, please consider leaving an honest review for it at your favorite online store.